# Jaci Burton

# Mountain Moonlight

## DEVLIN DYNASTY

ELLORA'S CAVE
ROMANTICA PUBLISHING

# *What the critics are saying...*

"Two very headstrong Alpha's battle wits, battle for control, and battle within themselves the heat generated between the two. Conner and Katya scorch the pages in this excellent addition to the Devlin Dynasty series. This book can be read independently but all the Devlin tales are yummy and well worth a look. Ms Burton did it again—a great book filled with emotions, tension and humor." ~ *The Romance Studio*

An Ellora's Cave Romantica Publication

www.ellorascave.com

Mountain Moonlight

ISBN 9781419952203
ALL RIGHTS RESERVED.
Mountain Moonlight Copyright © 2005 Jaci Burton
Edited by Briana St. James.
Cover art by Syneca.

Electronic book Publication January 2005
Trade paperback Publication July 2005

Excerpt from *Animal Instincts* Copyright © Jaci Burton, 2005

# Also by Jaci Burton

# About the Author

&

Jaci Burton has been a dreamer and lover of romance her entire life. Consumed with stories of passion, love and happily ever afters, she finally pulled her fantasy characters out of her head and put them on paper. Writing allows her to showcase the rainbow of emotions that result from falling in love.

Jaci lives in Oklahoma with her husband (her fiercest writing critic and sexy inspiration), stepdaughter and three wild and crazy dogs. Her sons are grown and live on opposite coasts and don't bother her nearly as often as she'd like them to. When she isn't writing stories of passion and romance, she can usually be found at the gym, reading a great book, or working on her computer, trying to figure out how she can pull more than twenty-four hours out of a single day.

Jaci welcomes comments from readers. You can find her website and email address on her author bio page at www.ellorascave.com.

## Tell Us What You Think
We appreciate hearing reader opinions about our books. You can email us at Comments@EllorasCave.com.

# MOUNTAIN MOONLIGHT
*Devlin Dynasty*

୬

# *Dedication*

*To Charlie, my alpha male, for giving me the kind of love
that I thought only existed in fiction.*

## Author's Note

The Carpathian Mountains are one of Europe's largest
mountain areas. Arching across seven countries in Central
Europe, from Austria to Ukraine and down to Romania, the
Carpathians are home to some 16 to 18 million people and key
refuge for Europe's largest populations of large carnivores
such as brown bear, wolf and lynx.

Though MOUNTAIN MOONLIGHT is a work of fiction,
the plight of wolves in the Carpathian mountain regions is
fact. The Carpathian Mountains are the last refuge for wolves
in Europe. Though much has been done to protect the
remaining wolves in Central Europe, they are still endangered.
Wolves know no borders, and crossing from one country to
another places them in potentially perilous situations. Despite
improvements made in protecting the wolf population of the
Carpathians, they are still hunted in many countries.

Fortunately, many conservation organizations exist
worldwide to protect the endangered wolf population,
including World Wildlife Federation (www.wwf.org) and
National Wildlife Federation (www.nwf.org).

# Chapter One
## *Vlasov, Romania*

ᔥ

The private car stopped in front of the Hotel Vlasov, the only modern hotel in a village that looked like something out of the past. Quaint medieval buildings were interspersed around a twin-towered, modern luxury hotel, a coming together of old and new all nestled in the tiny town situated at the foot of the Carpathian Mountains.

Conner Devlin sighed and shrugged his shoulders, tension knotting every muscle in his body. What a long damn flight followed by an equally lengthy car ride. If he didn't see the cramped confines of an airplane or vehicle for the next year, he'd be a happy man.

"'Bout damn time we got here."

Conner stretched, nodding at his brother, Noah. "I'm sick of travel."

"Ditto."

Hopefully they'd get their business out of the way fast so he could get back home.

The hotel was small, yet elegantly furnished with a Russian flair. Ornate wall hangings decorated the lobby, a combination of both modern and old-world with opulent gold-toned chairs sitting alongside chrome and glass tables.

The floor was beige and cream marble, slick and polished to a gleaming shine. Fading sunlight filtered in from the floor-to-ceiling windows, showcasing a dynamic view of the Carpathians.

By the time they checked in, the need to stretch out and run was like a fire burning inside him. He'd definitely need a trek into the nearby woods tonight.

But now the sun shone just above the tip of the mountains, its rays slicing through the clouds and reflecting off the green hillsides. He gazed up at the Carpathians. Somewhere up there was Braslieu castle. And within the property the Braslieu family owned were his kin.

Distant kin, but blood nonetheless. And Devlins protected their own. Otherwise he'd have never made this hellish trip.

He wrinkled his nose and blew out a tired breath.

Why did he have to come to Romania? Why couldn't one of his staff have done this instead? Christ, he'd drawn the short straw on this one.

His parents said he was needed here, that his research and development expertise made him the prime candidate to set up and manage the wildlife preserve.

Yeah, yeah, yeah. Still…Romania?

"Don't look so happy," Noah deadpanned.

Conner rolled his eyes, both annoyed and glad that his brother had come with him. Only a year apart in age, they had been friends more than brothers—tight, sharing everything, including their women on occasion. And also sparring on a regular basis, a pastime they both enjoyed way more than they'd ever admit. "What's there to be happy about? I haven't even been here an hour and I'm ready to go home."

"That's because you miss the women."

Ignoring Noah's smirk, Conner shrugged. "I can get women anywhere. I just hate international travel."

"And you miss the women."

This time Conner laughed. "Yeah, I miss the women."

Ah, the good life. He'd sure as hell miss it once he was forced to settle down, which hopefully wouldn't be anytime soon. Despite the fact his parents seemed hell-bent on sending every one of their offspring to different parts of the world in order to expand the pack, he'd been spared so far. Maybe it was his sister Chantal's turn now. His two older brothers, Jason and Max, had already been assigned to new locations. They'd also managed to find mates. Conner wasn't anywhere near ready to find a mate, and he knew damn well Noah was even less ready.

At least Noah had been sent to accompany him and provide protection. Besides, who better to do the tracking of the pack than Noah? It was his specialty and he was one of the best.

The bell captain brought their luggage by, indicating in stilted English that he'd be taking it to their rooms. Thank God a few people spoke English here.

A week to rest and check out the area would be nice. Not gonna happen, but would have been nice. They had to get started right away. Before the government intervened and they lost control of the pack.

"What time are we meeting Katya?" Noah asked.

"Seven tonight."

"What's her function in this deal?"

"She's the business manager for the Braslieu holdings and she'll be working with us to set up the preserve."

"Guess we should get unpacked and cleaned up, then," Noah grumbled, showing about as much enthusiasm for this project as Conner.

They had booked private cottages instead of the main building. Conner hated hotels. There was never any privacy. If he had to be here, at least he could have something that resembled a private apartment. The cottages were only a short walk from the hotel entrance, down a well-lit path into the forested area.

Now this was more like it. Though the pale stone cottages were nestled fairly close together, they were still separate dwellings. He slipped his key into the lock and stepped inside, flipping on the light and taking a look around.

Not bad. There was a living area complete with a desk where he could work, a kitchen and a separate, closed-off bedroom with a large bath. The bed was king-sized, thank God. Nothing like trying to fit his six-foot-two frame into a tiny double bed like a lot of hotels provided. He hated when his feet hung off the bed. And the bedroom had French doors leading out to a small terrace, complete with table, chairs and a spectacular view of the mountains. The moon rose opposite the mountains, and Conner immediately fell its pull.

Too bad he didn't have time to go for a run like he'd wanted to. But as he glanced at his watch he realized he didn't have much time to get ready before meeting Katya.

After he'd showered and dressed, he felt at least a little refreshed. Hopefully he'd be able to carry on a lucid conversation now, despite the jet lag. He left the cottage and met Noah coming out his door.

"Where?" Noah asked.

"Her cottage. She left the number with the front desk." Katya's cottage was behind his so it only took them a few seconds. He knocked and waited.

A distinctly female voice answered in rapid Romanian. Shortly the door swung open to a gorgeous vision.

Well, hell. Hadn't expected to be gut-punched in reaction, but that's exactly how he felt. An instantaneous, combustible response to the woman standing there.

Dressed in tight tan pants, brown suede boots and a full-length sweater, she was the most beautiful woman he'd ever seen. Creamy skin, silky black hair and eyes the color of rich brandy. Luscious, like the primal forests he loved, she had a wild look about her, encased within pristine beauty. She had a classic hourglass figure—perfect, full breasts, small waist and curvy hips, all leading down to very long legs.

Damn she was hot. And for some reason he'd expected a middle-aged, all business type of woman.

She licked her lips and arched her brow, her gaze lingering longer than he'd expected it to.

Eye contact with her was electric.

He inhaled, picking up her scent, a mixture of wildflowers and —

Lupine. Katya was lupine. His pulse kicked into gear and the change could have easily overtaken him as animal lust took over. If he hadn't practiced tamping down the urges for years, she'd be faced with one very horny werewolf right now.

"You are the Devlins, I presume?"

She welcomed them with a smile. Damn, that smile did something to his dick. The tiredness left his body now that she had his cock's full attention

Somehow managing to find his voice, he held out his hand. "Conner Devlin. This is my brother, Noah."

She nodded and shook both their hands. The contact with her skin was electrifying. When she pulled her hand away in a hurry, he knew she felt it, too.

"Come in."

Katya's voice was dark and rich, just like her beautiful eyes. She directed them to the chairs in the living room. "Something to drink? Brandy, perhaps?"

He nodded and she turned toward the kitchen, saying something in Romanian. In a few moments a tall blonde carried in a silver tray. The woman wore skin-tight leather pants and a low-cut red sweater. She was tall, reed-thin and absolutely gorgeous.

Conner sensed Noah's reaction. Hell, if he wasn't so mesmerized by Katya he'd probably have the same thoughts running through his head right now that Noah had. That blonde was edible.

"This is Elena, my cousin," Katya said. Elena nodded, her gaze lingering on Noah. Blue eyes darkened and she licked her lips, not even making an attempt to hide her lust.

Lucky Noah. Conner didn't even have to wager that his brother would get laid tonight.

A man stepped out of the kitchen. About his height, rugged-looking and burly, he looked a lot like a prizefighter. His nose was wide and slightly crooked and he had a menacing stare that any normal male would be wary of.

"This is Peter," Katya said.

Peter nodded and slipped into a spot on the sofa next to Katya. Conner noticed how Katya inched away from Peter. He also noticed the glare Peter gave her.

Interesting. Lovers, maybe? That thought irritated him, though he didn't know why. What difference did it make to him if Katya and Peter were fucking?

"I want to thank you both for coming in answer to our request for funding from the Devlin Foundation," Katya started. "It means a great deal to us that you are willing to assist us with setting up the wolf preserve."

"Your application and information were very enlightening," Conner said. "The Devlins had no idea that Carpathian wolves were in such danger."

Katya nodded. "It's not highly publicized. The government would like all the animal rights organizations to think they have a wolf-friendly policy, but the hunting organizations here have much influence over our government. It's imperative that we protect the wolves from them."

"Then I look forward to surveying the Braslieu estate. As we explained in our letter, we never make a final decision without a site inspection. That's primarily why we're here. We want to make sure the Devlin Foundation money is spent wisely and on valid causes."

"Of course."

She studied him, cocking her head to the side, her gaze traveling along his body. His jeans tightened as his cock came to life. When she inhaled, her breasts pressed against her sweater, her nipples outlined against the fabric.

A sudden urge to lift her sweater and press his mouth to those pebbled buds made the room much warmer.

*Focus on business. You're not here to fuck her.*

"What is your capacity with the Braslieu family?" he asked, noticing Elena and Peter's gazes flit to Katya as soon as he asked the question.

"I manage all business affairs for the family. As you are aware, the Braslieu castle is one of the oldest in Romania, with a rich history. However, the...principal family members are rather reclusive. They prefer business transactions occur using an intermediary. That's where I come in. I handle everything dealing with people outside the royal family."

So if Katya was lupine, did that mean the entire Braslieu population was, too? Despite extensive research, he couldn't find out much about the family other than there was a king and queen. It was like they were shrouded in some huge mystery and nobody was talking.

"We'd like to meet the royal family."

Katya shook her head. "Not possible. They do not meet with outsiders."

His first thought was to object. But he had to remember that he wasn't in Boston now and the rules of the game were different. He had to respect the family's need for privacy. And as long as Katya held some kind of power of attorney or authority to make business decisions for the family, that would have to suffice. "Very well. I don't like the idea of not meeting the king and queen, but I'll abide by their wishes. What are your plans for our visit?"

Katya exhaled, glad the first meeting went so smoothly. "We'll go over paperwork and funding for the next couple days. Then, if all that meets with your approval, we'll take you to the castle for a tour."

Conner nodded. "Sounds fine." He stood, nodded at Peter and Elena, then shook her hand. Heat shot through her body, a warm ache settling between her legs. She resisted the urge to squeeze her thighs together, wishing she were alone right now. The sudden urge to come had her legs trembling.

After the Devlins left, she looked to Elena and Peter. "I need to get some rest. I have a headache." Her comment was mainly for Peter and Elena would know that. The last thing she needed right now was him hanging around trying to convince her how great he was in bed. Grudgingly, he walked out.

Katya shut and bolted the door, finally letting out the breath she'd been holding. Frankly, she'd expected the Devlins to put up more of a fight over not meeting the royal family. Since it was Braslieu land the reserve would be built on, she was sure they'd insist.

Conner Devlin surprised her. In more ways than just readily agreeing to abide by family wishes. She hadn't expected to open the door to two breathtakingly handsome men. Men who exuded power and arrogance, whose lupine scent shocked her system into awakening for the first time in...

...ever, actually. She'd never felt a lupine sexual connection with a male before, even though she'd lived among them her entire life. Which was one of the reasons she remained a virgin, though not the most important reason. That had to do with power and control. A control she wouldn't give up to just any man. Only to her life mate — the first and only man she would share her body with.

She had thought by the time she reached her mid-twenties she'd have mated. Elena told her she was too picky. Katya felt Elena wasn't picky enough. But Elena didn't have as much at stake as Katya did. Giving up her virginity meant so much more than just simple desire and release. There were political ramifications to her choice of a mate. Many of the pack had attempted to seduce her. All had failed.

One refused to give up. Peter.

Which was his problem, not hers. She'd told Peter on more than one occasion they would never be mated. Peter just had a problem with taking no for an answer, convinced she'd someday change her mind about him.

Not likely. Peter's arrogance wasn't borne of confidence. He had a high opinion of himself and wore his conceit like a valued prize, thinking women would drop their panties for him every time he blinked his chocolate brown eyes in their direction.

Maybe other women, but never her. She felt nothing for him and the sooner he accepted that, the better.

Katya wouldn't mate with anyone she didn't choose herself. And she didn't make that choice lightly. To rule beside her would require a strong mate, one who could take care of all the people of Braslieu. She'd yet to find a man like that. No one had ever stirred her mind, her heart and her body.

She shook off her thoughts and forced herself to focus on the project at hand. Now that the initial meeting was over, she had time to settle back and figure out how to handle the Devlins.

They could never find out about her and what role she actually played in the Braslieu family. That would have to remain a mystery, as it was to everyone outside the pack. Royalty were treated differently than common people. She hated that, which was why no one outside the castle knew who she was.

The business arrangements between the Devlin Foundation and the Braslieu family would be best conducted between business associates.

They had to provide funding for the shelter. They had to. The family, while royal, possessed no funds. Their near bankruptcy was a closely guarded secret, and one which she wouldn't use as a point of negotiation. The Braslieus had never begged for money before and wouldn't start now. But the safety of all the Carpathian wolves was at stake here, and the government offered no assistance in keeping the hunters from the wolves. Without the help of a wildlife preservation organization such as the Devlin's, their future looked dismal.

Katya stood and stretched her back, feeling the need for air. The room seemed to close in on her more each minute. The cottages here were nothing like home. She missed the spacious rooms where she could pace end to end and think.

Grabbing her jacket, she stepped outside, sucking in life-affirming night air. Cool air swirled around her, easing the burdens she carried. Outside she felt part of nature. The pack called to her senses, reminding her of her responsibility.

She'd die to protect them, to assure their continuity.

A cold north wind blew against her face as she walked the long path to the edge of the mountain. Once inside the narrow thicket of trees, she stopped to look up at the quarter moon drifting in and out of the clouds, its lunar force tugging inside her. The urge to run was great. To go home, right now, and hide. The white fog of her breath was visible in the chilled night as she let out a sigh.

If there was any other way to do this she'd never bring outsiders in. But there wasn't. She'd exhausted every option. Yes, the Devlins were strangers, but she'd researched their charitable foundations and was impressed. The work they did with wolves, especially, interested her.

And no wonder, considering she'd scented both Conner and Noah as lupine. But there was something else, too. When she'd met Conner Devlin she was struck by a feeling of…

…destiny.

Not one to fall for a handsome face and utterly delectable male physique, she nevertheless had to pick up her tongue and tuck it inside her mouth when she'd caught her first glimpse of him.

Very tall, well-muscled, with strong arms, broad shoulders and powerful, long legs. Despite the jeans and heavy shirt he wore, she could see the strong body underneath.

And she wanted.

For the first time in her life, she wanted. Her body had reacted violently, surging to life with a vengeance. Her breasts felt heavy and tight, her nipples pebbling and throbbing with an unfamiliar ache. And her sex had opened, moistened, immediately ready for a cock.

Such a physical reaction had never happened before, especially around a stranger. But there was just something about Conner Devlin that called to her.

Kindred spirits? Or the kind she should be wary of?

"There's nothing like the moon, is there?"

In the split second before he'd spoken she'd sensed him behind her, so his voice didn't surprise her. But she couldn't allow her mind and body to wander in thoughts of him. Conner Devlin was already a distraction she couldn't afford.

She turned and nodded. "Yes, the moon is very special."

Did he know about her as she knew about him? She wouldn't volunteer the information, preferring instead for him to mention it. After all, not every lupine had developed the ability to discern a human shifter.

"What are you doing out here?" she asked.

He shrugged. "I was going to ask you the same thing."

"I'm restless when away from home."

"I understand that sentiment completely."

They stared at the moon together for a while, wrapped in a silence that should have been uncomfortable, but wasn't.

"So tell me, Katya, how is it that you speak such fluent English?"

"I went to college in America."

He arched a brow. "Really? Where?"

"University of New York."

"Degree?"

"Biology. And you?"

"Did my undergrad and graduate work at Boston University. Business."

"I see. A good education for your job, then."

"You could say that."

"Do you travel often on behalf of the Devlin Foundation?"

"I do the occasional site visit, but my staff usually handles those."

"Then why are you and your brother here instead of your staff?"

"The Devlins thought it an important enough venture that the principals should be here to oversee."

Was that good or bad? "So you're the decision maker, the most important of the Devlins."

His lips curled in a smile that was both compelling and dangerous. "You could say that. I'll be the one who'll make the final decision on funding your refuge."

His confident arrogance should have irritated her. Instead, she admired it. She'd never found followers to be particularly appealing, yet had never seen an alpha leader in action before.

Except her father. And that had been a long time ago.

There was nothing wrong in fighting for what you really wanted. It was the way of her people, and it was her way. She'd done battle and taken her war to protect the wolves to the very edge many times. Giving up had never been an option.

"Do you have a family, Katya? Husband, children?"

Family. Her throat constricted and she pushed the memories aside. "No. My parents are both dead. I have no husband. Although I have a rather large...extended family. And you?"

"My parents live in Boston. I have three brothers, a sister and a lot of extended family members here and there."

"That must be nice."

"I take it you have no siblings, then?"

"No. None at all." Loneliness surrounded her, the memories thickening like the evening fog. Conner moved in front of her, forcing her gaze away from the mountains onto him. His eyes were like the sky in the winter. Crisp, cool, and utterly mesmerizing.

Her mind screamed danger, her body warmed so fast and so hot she wanted to remove her coat and let the cold air slap some sense into her. This physical reaction to Conner was unnerving and unexpected. She had to keep her distance from him. "I think we've talked enough tonight. I'm very tired."

She turned to walk away, but his hand shot out and grasped her upper arm. Heat burned through her coat and layers of clothing. Unfamiliar urges washed over her. Arousal, desire, want. The need to mate had never reared up before, but primal urges pummeled her.

Why now, and why with this man?

"You're a woman of great mystery, Katya. I like that."

Her throat went dry and she struggled to swallow past the lump forming there. She had no experience with men, didn't really know how to handle a sexual attraction that had materialized out of nowhere. He stood so close to her that if she inhaled deeply her breasts would brush his chest.

The thought of rubbing her nipples against his naked chest nearly sent her to her knees. She fought to still the trembling of her limbs. A deep need to feel the contact of skin against skin, fur against fur, enveloped her. She began to perspire, suddenly too hot for all the clothing she wore.

"I love uncovering a mystery. How about you?"

She searched for words, anything to break the spell he'd woven over her normal sensibilities. "Mysteries can be dangerous."

He nodded and pulled her closer, wrapping his arms around her waist and drawing her against his body. "I like dangerous. Do you like dangerous, Katya?"

Her body screamed yes. She wanted danger, wanted to strip off her clothing and run as far and fast as she could, hoping that Conner would give chase.

She wanted the challenge, and the reward at the end.

She wanted him.

Desires like that could be perilous. "There's no place for danger in my life, Conner. We have a business relationship and we should keep it at that."

He paused, his hold on her loosening. But then he shook his head, smiled and said, "I don't think I want to. Do you really want to keep your distance from me, Katya?"

With utter fascination she watched his mouth draw ever closer to hers.

By the time his breath caressed her cheek, her lips had parted and she was ready for him. When his mouth descended gently but firmly over hers, her world shattered in a million pieces. His tongue parted the seam of her lips and slipped inside, gently probing. She sighed, shivered and melted in his arms.

# Chapter Two

ഇ

Conner felt like he'd been slammed against a wall and had the breath knocked from him. Katya sure as hell wasn't the first woman he'd kissed, but she was the first one to make him feel dizzy and harden him in an instant.

Her body fit perfectly against his, her soft belly tucked against his hip, her thigh pressed against his throbbing erection.

She moaned and snuggled closer, wrapping her arms around his shoulders and leaning intimately against him, opening her mouth for his tongue.

He entered the dark, moist recesses of her mouth as if he'd been waiting a lifetime for this. Her lips were warm, sweet, inviting him to explore. Needing no further urging, he plunged his tongue in again, teasing her with the promise of something wild and untamed.

She trembled in his arms. But it wasn't from the cold. Even with the layers of clothing between them, she was a raging inferno that flamed his senses.

A part of him wondered what the hell he was doing, entwined in a passionate embrace with a business associate. Katya was a mystery. Maybe that was the appeal.

No, that wasn't quite right. The appeal was her pliant, lush body sliding against him, the woman scent of her, aroused and spiked with the perfume of sweetest jasmine. The way her mouth followed the movements of his, the tentative way she slid her tongue against his, almost as if she'd never…

She shifted, her sex brushing against his hard thigh, and he lost all train of thought. Accommodating her need, he slid one jean-clad leg between hers until his thigh made contact with her cunt.

The thin leggings she wore offered no barrier. Her pussy scalded his leg and made him burn in another way, a way that had him doing the trembling now.

He'd never wanted a woman so desperately before.

Tugging the zipper of her parka, he yanked it down and slipped his hand inside, searching for the hem of her sweater. His lips still claimed hers, his tongue continuing to dive inside and taste her sweet mouth.

At last he made contact with the hot, bare skin of her belly, feeling it quiver under his questing fingers. He drew the sweater up with the movements of his hand, searching and finding one soft globe unhindered by a bra. Thank God. He'd have had to rip the damn thing off with his teeth if he'd encountered it.

When his palm brushed her erect nipple, she gasped, jerked her head away and stared into his eyes.

Her eyes were glazed with passion, her lips swollen from his kisses. The flush of her cheeks screamed her arousal. She rocked against his thigh and hissed.

In response to her unspoken request, he plucked at the nipple and she sucked in her bottom lip, tugging at it with her teeth as if she fought the sensations hammering away at her. Grasping her buttocks, he moved her against his leg. She threw her head back, revealing the smooth column of her neck. Christ, he could spend hours licking and nibbling at her slender throat. Her lips parted and she panted heavily, her whispered cries driving him near mad with lust.

He'd had plenty of spontaneous sex with women before, but nothing like this bonfire of sensation Katya had awakened within him. What was it about her that called to him in such a primitive way?

"Come on, baby, let go," he urged, moving his thigh against her hot pussy.

Eyes widening, she tilted her head forward and clutched his shoulders, riding his leg hard and fast until she shivered and cried out. He captured her moans with his mouth, plunging his tongue between her parted lips and drinking in the sounds and movements as she climaxed.

Tears filled her eyes as she rode out her orgasm. She collapsed against his chest, panting heavily.

As his nostrils drew in the scent of her creamy release, his balls drew tight, his cock searching relentlessly for escape from its confines.

Shit, he needed to fuck her right here, right now, and didn't care who saw them.

He wanted this woman.

"Katya," he started, but before he could say any more she pulled away from his embrace and shook her head.

With trembling fingers she zipped her parka, her cheeks turning pink. She didn't even make eye contact with him, instead spoke to his chest. "Oh, God. I'm...I'm so sorry. I can't do this, Conner."

*Okay. Step back and breathe. The lady is having second thoughts.* Trying for a smile she refused to see, he said, "I think you just did."

Her eyes closed and heat flushed her face and neck. "That wasn't me. Well, it was, but... Oh, God, I'm so sorry." She dragged her hands through her hair and looked at the ground.

"Sure felt like you." *And smelled like you, tasted like you.* And he wanted so much more than that brief teasing glimpse of her passion. He wanted to sink so far inside her he forgot who he was.

"It was a mistake and I can't do this. We shouldn't do this. We have business to conduct and this...well, it just can't happen."

"Why not?"

"It just can't. It's not you, it's me. I can't explain. I'm sorry, Conner. I have to go."

He knew from the tense grit of her teeth and the way she clenched her jaw that she had as little control as he right now. He could drag her into the nearby woods and fuck her until they both screamed their release.

He wanted that more than anything.

What stopped him was the fear and wariness he read in her eyes, and the sudden realization that Katya wasn't very experienced with sex.

How he knew that he wasn't certain. He just knew. And while fucking Katya would be enjoyable, it could also really complicate his job here.

Glancing quickly at him, she shook her head and turned away. Instead of following her, he stood and watched her hurry toward her cottage, admiring the way her backside swayed.

Shuddering with pent-up arousal, he forced his thoughts away from immediate sexual gratification and fought to gain control over his libido.

When he felt like he could actually walk again, he made the trek back to his room, knowing he'd get no sleep tonight.

* * * * *

Katya took a long swallow of brandy, then shuddered as the liquid burned its way down her throat. Though she doubted the alcohol would help her sleep. Not after what had happened tonight with Conner

How could she sleep? Her body throbbed, her sex wept with need and desire and her nipples were so sensitive that wearing clothes was painful. Riding his leg to orgasm had been exquisite, yet not nearly enough to satisfy her.

What had she been thinking, letting herself go like that? Her actions were uncharacteristic. Completely unlike her. She knew what was at stake when she got involved with a man. Conner Devlin was a business partner, and a stranger at that. Yet she'd thrown herself at him like a woman starving for male attention.

She set the glass down and stood, crossing her arms in front of her and pacing the living room, trying to bury the embarrassment, the self-disgust, as far down as it would go.

What would have happened if Conner hadn't immediately backed away when she said no? She'd have compromised him, for certain, and by custom forced him into a mating he wouldn't want.

Of course he wouldn't want her, other than as a random fuck. They were strangers and nothing more.

But she'd come close to screwing up both their lives. In the future she'd have to be more careful. Her body was primed for mating, and for some strange reason it had chosen Conner as the one.

Ridiculous. Her mate would be her choice, not something conjured up by lupine hormones and the moon. She'd heard that oftentimes a mate was destined, that the one person you know you have to spend the rest of your life with was preordained, and once you met, neither heaven nor hell could stop the mating.

But that was folklore. Her problem was the fact she should have had sex a long time ago and she'd held out. Her body was tired of waiting.

Too bad.

She looked up when she heard the knock at the door, glancing at the clock and frowning. It was one in the morning. Who the hell could it be? Elena had wandered off with Noah, no doubt in the woodland somewhere fucking their brains out.

Her first thought was Conner, but then she dismissed it. Why would he come to her room in the middle of the night? She'd made it clear that what happened between them was a mistake.

"Who is it?" she asked at the door.

"Peter."

Oh, God. Not now. "It's late. What do you want?"

"It's important, Katya. I need to talk to you."

She jerked open the door, intending to tell him that unless there was some kind of crisis, she wasn't going to allow him in. "Whatever it is can wait until—"

He pushed his way in and shut the door behind him, his face twisted in rage.

"What the hell do you think you're doing?"

"I saw you with him tonight."

His eyes glowed with anger. Her heart slammed against her chest. "What are you talking about?"

"That Devlin bastard. What the fuck were you thinking, throwing yourself on him like that?"

Embarrassment flamed her, but indignation quickly took over. How dare he interfere in her private life? This claim he felt he had on her had to end. She pushed at his chest. "I did *not* throw myself on him, and even if I had, what I do is none of your damn business. Now get out!"

Peter grabbed her wrist and turned her around, twisting her arm behind her back. Shock heated her body, tears springing to her eyes as pain shot through her arm. He growled into her ear. "I presume whatever the fuck I want to. You're mine, Katya. No man will ever have you but me. As I suspected, you need me around to keep you in line."

This wasn't happening. What had gotten into him? "You're hurting me, dammit! Let me go, Peter, before you do something you will regret."

She'd heard this conversation over and over again from him, but he'd never acted this violently. Her arm ached, her shoulder stretched so tight she felt like it would pop out of its socket if he didn't let loose soon.

"You need a mate. Someone to dominate you."

She shuddered in revulsion when his tongue snaked out and swiped her neck. "You need a cold shower and a fuck with some other woman," she countered. "Because you're *never* going to get that from me!"

"Won't I? I think it's long past time I force the issue. You will be mine, if I have to fuck you without your consent."

She stilled. He wouldn't do that. She'd tell everyone he raped her. Though it wouldn't matter at that point. Once he took her, she would be forever bound to him.

And he knew that. Had he become so desperate to have her he was willing to resort to rape?

*Don't do this, Peter. Don't ruin both our lives.*

He pushed her forward, heading for the bedroom. Okay, time to think. She had to clear her head. She had to force herself to relax, calm down and stem the panic that bubbled up in her suddenly dry throat. She had to think this through, figure out how to stop him before it was too late.

As a human she was no match for him. Peter was much taller and stronger. But as a wolf, she'd stand a better chance of either wounding him in some way or maneuvering her way free so she could run.

"Peter, stop this. You don't want me this way."

His voice was barely recognizable, dripping with sarcasm. "I'll take you any way I can get you. With or without your consent. Trust me, Katya. You'll like it. I'm good, baby. Really, really good. I'll have you whimpering to come in no time at all."

The visuals conjured up by his words made her nauseous. But she let him push her down the hall, relaxing against him as if she'd given up the fight and would go along with him now.

In response, he loosened his hold, enough that when he laid her down on the bed she forced the shift. Her teeth elongated first and before he had a chance to pin her down, she sank them deep into his arm.

31

Peter screamed and yanked his arm away. "You bitch! You'll pay for that!"

She scrambled off the bed but he caught her hair before she could escape the bedroom. Tears filled her eyes as he dragged her back by her ponytail, then threw her to the floor, shifting partially so that his strength overpowered her. Pulling his arm back, he struck her across the face, his unsheathed claws tearing into her skin. An explosion rocked her temporarily blind. Searing fire burned along her temple and cheek, rendering her momentarily dazed.

While she fought for clarity, he sat on top of her middle and began to tear at her clothes.

No! No, no, no! This was *not* going to happen!

Dizziness pounded at her and she struggled to keep Peter's face in focus. Warm liquid oozed down her neck. She didn't need to touch it to know it was blood.

He ripped her shirt open, reaching for her breasts and squeezing them so hard that pain shot through her.

"You're going to pay for making me wait," he growled. "And for riding that bastard Devlin instead of me!"

She wished she was still dressed instead of just her long shirt and underwear. He quickly tore her panties, reaching for the zipper of his pants and yanking it down.

Bile rose up in her throat and she was afraid she'd throw up. She was too angry to feel the fear. Too livid to just lie there and let him rape her. No way was she giving up without a fight. She tamped down the nausea and continued to force her body to change, her strength growing more with each passing second.

It was a race to see which one of them could complete the transformation first, since he could easily take her in wolf form, too. Her fingernails became claws and she lashed out at him with wolf strength, pushing him off long enough to scramble onto her haunches and tear into his upper arm with her teeth. Peter screamed, but his rage made him stronger and he jumped back on top of her, flipping her over onto her stomach and pressing his knee into her upper back.

She couldn't breathe! He'd cut off her oxygen, the shock delaying her ability to completely change. But he'd had plenty of time, nearly half shifted now and growing in strength.

"I want to take you like this. Human to human. I want to hear you scream when I sink my cock into you."

"I won't scream for you, you sonofabitch," she managed between gasping breaths. "And if you rape me, you will suffer the consequences," she bit back, her teeth clenched in an effort to force him off her.

His laughter spoke of near hysteria. "I know the laws here as well as you. Lupine law supersedes human and you know that. Now spread your legs so I can take what's mine."

She'd die fighting him before she ever let him touch her. She'd just wait him out again, relax enough that he'd let down his guard. Only this time she'd go for his throat.

But when she felt the tip of his cock against her buttocks, she began to worry. If he succeeded in penetrating her, all was lost. He could rightly claim her as his.

Sweat poured from her as she fought. Her skin burned where his claws dug in to hold her down. When he growled and ripped into her shoulder with his teeth, she knew she had to do something now. But she couldn't breathe with his weight on top of her. Without air, she couldn't struggle, couldn't fight.

Goddamn it! She hated being a woman.

Peter would pay for this. Somehow, someway, if she had to kill the prick herself, he'd pay for what he was about to do. She gritted her teeth and prepared to fight him, no matter the outcome.

Suddenly, his weight on her eased, then disappeared.

She sucked in a breath, oxygen filling her compressed lungs, then flipped over, stunned to see Conner snarling at Peter as he held him in a chokehold. Peter dug his claws into Conner's forearm in an effort to pull him off. Despite the fact the men were about equal in size, Conner controlled him as if he was a small pup.

Katya struggled to stand, then dragged the cover off the bed and wrapped it around herself. Exhausted from that slight effort, she flopped onto the edge of the bed, her limbs shaking too hard to stand.

"Are you all right?" Conner asked, still maintaining his hold on Peter.

Her throat was dry and she was near tears, hating her body's reaction to this event. She nodded and croaked out, "Yes."

Conner turned his attention to Peter, squeezing Peter's throat tighter. "When a woman says no, it means no," Conner snarled. "Haven't you ever learned that?"

"She's mine!" Peter choked, his face red with fury. "She's always been mine."

Conner's lethal smile was unnerving. As was his calm voice when he said, "Didn't look to me like she was yours. In fact, what happened in here looks suspiciously like attempted rape."

Peter stilled. "You have no authority here. Stay out of our business."

"I'm here, and I'm knee-deep in your business, dumbass. Pay real close attention because I'm only going to say this once. You touch her again—I'll kill you."

"And I said—"

Peter's next words were cut off because Conner growled, his claws extending further until a line of red appeared at Peter's throat, precariously close to a vital artery. "Are you listening now?"

Katya couldn't resist the upward curve of her lips as Peter finally stopped struggling. His eyes looked like they were going to pop out of his head, his cheeks red and puffed out as he struggled to speak. "Yes. I hear you!"

Noah tore through the doorway, skidding to a halt. His gaze darted in all directions of the room, quickly assessing what move to make first. "Got everything under control in here?"

Conner nodded, his face and body returning to human state. "Yeah. Take this scum and lock him up somewhere until I've had a chance to talk to Katya."

Noah glanced over at Katya. Seeing the horror and anger on his face, she resisted the urge to smooth her tangled hair away from her face and wipe the blood from her cheek. She had to look a lot worse than she felt.

Then again, she felt pretty bad right now. "Is Elena with you?" she asked Noah.

"She was earlier, but then she left, saying she was going in to town to meet some friends and she'd be out the rest of the night."

Katya nodded. Elena knew many people in the valley and often stopped off to visit with them. She wouldn't be back until morning.

"You need me to go find her?" Noah asked.

Managing a smile despite the shooting pain in her cheek, she shook her head. "No, I'll be fine. Just get *him* out of my room."

"Gladly. Come on, prick. Doesn't take a rocket scientist to figure out what happened in here tonight. You're lucky Conner found you first. He's much nicer than I am. Otherwise you'd be dead by now."

Noah dragged Peter from the room. As soon as they were out of eyesight, her shoulders slumped and she began to shake, hating to show weakness in front of Conner but unable to prevent the physiological reaction to the attack. One of the drawbacks to being partially human—dealing with human biological functions.

And now a stranger tended to her. He sat next to her on the bed, looking as uncomfortable as she felt. Twice he lifted his hand as if he'd wrap his arm around her, then settled it down at his side again. Tension tightened the muscles of his thigh as it brushed against hers.

"Let me go get someone from the hotel to help you."

He stood but she reached for his arm. "Please don't. I don't want anyone to know." Calling attention to herself was never a good idea. And being lupine meant the hotel doctor couldn't be called in. Since Conner was well aware of that fact, she knew he wouldn't offer to fetch the physician.

He studied her, then nodded. "Tell me what you need."

Grateful he hadn't tried to treat her like a helpless woman, she said, "I'll be fine here alone."

"No, you're not going to be alone. I know enough about trauma to realize that's the last thing you need. You're injured. How about we start by cleaning you up and assessing the damage?"

She was almost afraid to look, but Conner was right. As it was, she could barely stand up.

"Any bones broken?"

She shook her head.

"Where does it hurt?"

Turning her head to look at him, she said, "Everywhere."

He grimaced. "Looks like it. Noah's right. I should have killed him."

"You made the right choice. My people will deal with him in their own way."

"Can you stand?"

She nodded. "Might need some help. My legs won't stop shaking."

"That's just a fight-or-flight reaction. From the looks of you, I'd say you put up one hell of a fight."

The pride in his voice made her smile. "I tried. Sonofabitch was bigger than me."

"Which is why he should have never forced himself on you like that. Goddamn it! It pisses me off when men get their rocks off by overpowering women."

He slid his hands under her arms and lifted her to a standing position, then let her lean on him as they moved into the bathroom. He seated her on the ample corner of the tub.

"Sit here. I'm going to run a bath for you and see if we can't eliminate some of the bloodstains."

We? What the hell did he mean by "we"? She watched him turn on the faucets and test the water temperature, then rummage through the bath salts on the edge of the tub. "This isn't quite muscle relaxing, but it'll do," he said, pouring some lavender salts under the tap water.

The smell of lavender shortly filled the room, relaxing her enough that her legs stopped shaking. "I think I can take it from here."

But instead of leaving, he crossed his arms and shook his head. "I'm not leaving you alone, and since your cousin's not here, you're stuck with me."

"I'm not bathing with you in the room."

"Yeah, you are, because I'm not leaving you alone."

His voice was commanding, yet gentle. Not at all like Peter's show of power. The fact he didn't coddle her or treat her like a victim was comforting. He was just...here. And that helped. Much as she'd rather have crawled into bed and pulled the covers over her head until she healed, Conner was right. She needed to clean up and assess the damage, at least estimate how long before the lupine part of her healed her body.

When the bath was full, Conner shut off the water and turned to her. "Drop the blanket and get in. I'll hold onto your hands for support."

Oh hell. He'd already seen her naked when he flew into the room and pulled Peter off her. She wasn't at her most attractive right now, though. Funny how that annoyed her. She dropped the blanket and reached for his hands, grateful for his strength as she wobbled a little lifting her leg over the edge of the tub. Conner squeezed her hands and stepped behind her, nestling his body against hers for support.

Nice. Hard, well-muscled body, she thought, then wondered how she could even think of a man's body after what she'd been through. It was probably a good sign, though, because it meant she was already beginning to heal.

Katya kept her gaze focused on the bathwater instead of on Conner, not wanting to see the reaction in his eyes. Would he cringe over the bruises that covered half her body? Damn, she'd fought harder than she thought judging from her injuries. And they hurt like hell, the cuts burning in the hot water. She settled in, laid her head against the cool back of the tub and closed her eyes.

Her eyes flew open when she felt something soft and warm against her injured cheek, only to find Conner had rolled up his shirtsleeves and was on his knees, leaning over the tub to press a washcloth to her face.

He smelled good. Not like cologne. Like soap. And man. Pure, sexy, his natural scent soaking into her senses.

"Does this hurt?" he asked, tenderly wiping the dried blood from her face.

"No." It felt good, actually. Getting Peter's scent off her was paramount. Despite the shock she knew she should feel, anger permeated her every thought. How dare Peter try to take what she hadn't offered?

She lay still while Conner washed her face and neck. Despite the fact he could see into the water, he didn't once glance down at her body. Instead, he focused on the areas he was cleaning. When he left and brought back a large bowl, then proceeded to lather up her hair and rinse it with clear water from the sink, she felt more like she'd been spending a day at a spa than recovering from a brutal attack.

"I think we got all the blood cleaned up. You ready to get out of there?"

She nodded and he lifted her, immediately wrapping a large bath towel around her. He held her hand as she stepped from the tub.

"Tell me where your nightgown is."

"Nightgown? I don't own any."

"What do you sleep in?"

"Usually, nothing. Unless it's really cold outside. Then I put on socks."

His eyes flamed for a brief second, then returned to normal again. "Here, wear this."

Now it was her turn to stare as he pulled off his long-sleeved shirt and took off the dark blue T-shirt underneath it. "It's clean. I just slipped it on after my shower, right before I heard the noises in here and ran in."

She was such an idiot! "I didn't even thank you for coming to help me."

"Not necessary. I'm glad I made it in time."

So was she, for reasons she couldn't explain.

He held his shirt out for her and she dropped the towel, his gaze flitting on her breasts for only a second before he met her eyes again. This time, that smoldering heat stayed around a little longer.

And she felt that heat. Felt it, and wondered how she could possibly feel attraction to someone after what she'd just been through.

She slipped his T-shirt over her head. It still held the warmth and smell of his body and she wanted to pull it closer against her skin.

"Again, thank you. Most people don't get involved in others' business. Most would have ignored the noises."

Reaching for his long-sleeved shirt, he shrugged into it and began to button it. "I'm not most people."

She was beginning to realize that.

# Chapter Three

೫

Conner poured two glasses of brandy, taking a moment to get his emotions under control before he stepped back into the room with Katya.

He still wanted to kill that sonofabitch. When he heard Katya's screams, he tore down the path and ripped open her front door, shocked to find Peter straddling her and ready to rape her. Blind rage filled him and he wanted to tear the lupine apart piece by piece. Instead, he'd forced common sense into his anger-soaked brain and lifted Peter off her bruised and bloody body, though he was perversely satisfied that she'd managed to wound the bastard a little.

The urge to choke the life from him still thundered through his blood.

Weak men preyed on women. As a lupine, Peter was considered a danger. Any other pack would kill him. But Conner had to respect the lupine laws of the Braslieus. He could only hope Peter would receive the justice he deserved.

Staying on to help Katya bathe had been a lesson in frustration. But what was he supposed to do? He couldn't leave her alone. She'd obviously needed help. Yes, she was lupine and she'd heal, but they all healed at different speeds. And she was damn well battered. He'd had no choice but to stay and help her.

Not that it was a hardship. His thoughts hadn't once strayed toward the sexual arena.

Okay, maybe once. Or twice. Oh hell, his dick had been hard the entire time he'd bathed her. Despite the blood and bruise marks on her body, she was beautiful. Tough, yet vulnerable.

*Quit thinking. It'll only get you in trouble.*

He grasped the snifters of brandy along with the bottle and carried them into the living room. Katya sat snuggled in the corner of the sofa with a blanket wrapped around her legs. They'd compromised on the sofa after she refused to go to bed, saying she needed to sit up for a while, that she couldn't possibly sleep right now. Even though she'd told him she felt fine and he could leave, something prevented him from doing so.

Peter wouldn't be back to bother her tonight. Conner knew Noah would keep a watchful eye over him. But still, he felt compelled to stay.

She looked up as he approached, managing a tremulous smile. She was already starting to heal, the lupine recuperative powers working quickly. The massive gash along her cheek was no more than a faint red line now. By morning it would be gone. The bruises along her arms, neck and face were fading.

Katya was one strong woman. Most would have crumbled under an assault like that, even a lupine. But she had a steel backbone, showing more anger than fear. He admired her for that.

"How do you feel?" he asked, handing her the snifter.

She took a sip and licked her bottom lip. His cock twitched.

"Better. Thank you. You really don't have to stay."

"I know I don't. I want to." He took a long swallow, hoping the fiery liquid would numb his libido. Lusting after a woman who'd just suffered a near-rape wasn't a good idea. The last thing he wanted to do was frighten her or have her doubt his reason for staying.

She didn't look scared, though. Instead, she studied him with clear, thoughtful eyes that heated him from the inside out. "Tell me about Peter."

She shrugged and finished off the brandy in two gulps. Her eyes watered and she shook it off. "He's a pain in the ass."

Conner laughed and refilled her glass. "Obviously. Has he tried anything like this before?"

"No. I've known him my entire life. He's a year older than me and we used to play together as children. Then when I returned home after college, he made it known he wanted to mate."

"You obviously didn't want that."

"No, I didn't. He didn't seem to care what I wanted. He was convinced I'd change my mind. But I never expected him to go this far."

"I wonder what triggered it tonight?"

She blushed and looked down at her lap before meeting his gaze again. "He told me he saw you and me together."

Ah, that explained the reason for Peter's rage. Jealousy. "So he decided since you were willing to give it up to me, he'd just show you who was boss."

She arched a brow. "I don't know about my willingness to 'give it up to you', but yes, I think he was jealous enough to stop asking and start taking."

"What do you mean you don't know?" She sure as hell seemed willing earlier. Then again, she had stopped him.

After draining her second glass of brandy, she said, "What happened earlier tonight between us was a mistake."

Was that her honest opinion, or embarrassment? "I didn't think it was a mistake at all."

She grabbed the bottle of brandy and splashed more into her glass. "Come on, Conner. You and I have a business relationship right now. Sex would only complicate that."

"True. But it doesn't stop me from wanting to make love to you."

Katya hitched a gasp as his words penetrated, hotter than the brandy burning its way through her body.

Dammit! She wasn't supposed to feel desire. Not now, not for him. But she couldn't stop her traitorous body from wanting what she shouldn't want, what she couldn't have.

Maybe it was the brandy. Maybe more of it would dull the ache of need she felt for Conner. She took a long, deep swallow and exhaled.

She normally didn't drink. Not more than a glass here and there. Yet the brandy went down smooth and easy, creating a lovely, fog-like haze around memories of a night filled with harsh reality. Her muscles relaxed, her bones feeling like they'd melted around her. She sank deeper into the couch and kicked the blanket aside, feeling too hot to be encumbered.

"Why don't you have someone in your life, Katya?" he asked.

"What?"

He finished his drink and set it on the table. "Look at you. You're young, beautiful, intelligent and desirable as hell. You must have men panting after you all the time. Why haven't you mated yet?"

She laughed, the fuzzy feeling in her head deliciously enticing. "I guess I haven't found the right one yet. I don't give men those kinds of signals. I'm just not interested in any of the ones I know."

He arched a brow. "You sure as hell gave me one tonight. Why?"

Memories of what they'd done drifted over her like a dip in a warm, scented pool. She took another drink of brandy, realizing she'd already consumed way more than she should. But she liked this feeling of numbness. "I don't know what happened tonight. I just... I don't know."

Why couldn't she form a coherent sentence? And why did the room suddenly seem so much smaller? She stared at Conner through brandy-soaked eyes, feeling the heat penetrate her sex. Her pussy throbbed.

No, wait. She didn't want Conner Devlin. But she couldn't remember why. There didn't seem to be a good enough reason to have walked away from him.

"Do I scare you, Katya?"

She frowned. "No. Not at all."

"Then why did you run earlier?"

Hell if she could remember why. Had to be the brandy obliterating her brain cells. Nothing seemed clear anymore. Forgetting everything seemed to be a really good idea right now.

"I don't know why. All I know is I don't want to run anymore." That much was true. She was tired of running, tired of waiting, tired of others making decisions for her. Why couldn't she have what she wanted, when she wanted it?

"Tell me what you want," he said, his voice a warm, comfortable lifeline. "Let me give you what you need."

Maybe it was remnants of Peter's touch that made her want to give Conner an honest answer. She wanted to erase the feel of Peter's hands on her, of his body pressed intimately against her, and replace it with Conner's hands, mouth and body. She wanted to take that feeling of helplessness and toss it right out the window, replace it with the power of her own choice.

She knew exactly what she wanted. For the first time in her life, she wanted control over her destiny. And this hazy place between fantasy and reality was a perfect start.

"I want you, Conner. I want you to touch me, to take away any traces of Peter that linger on my body or in my mind, and replace it with memories of you."

His eyes went golden, glowing like a bright flame. "I think that's the brandy talking."

Everyone always seemed to think they knew what was best for her. She reached for him, scooting closer until her bare thigh brushed his jean-clad leg. The contact was electric, arcing between her legs so fast and furiously she wanted to slide her hand there and increase the intensity. "No, it's me talking. I do know what I want, Conner. Please don't make me ask again."

Maybe he wasn't interested after what happened tonight. Some men blamed the woman for a rape or attempted rape, as if she'd somehow led them on. Is that how Conner felt?

But he reached for her chin, tipping it up so her gaze met his. She didn't see condemnation in his eyes; she saw raw, untamed desire. "I don't want to hurt you. I want you, Katya, so damn bad my cock aches. But you have to call the shots and tell me exactly how, when and how hard you want it."

Oh, God. How. When. How hard. Her entire body tingled with anticipation. She'd never wanted anything as desperately as she wanted him. "I'm not very…experienced. Show me."

Jesus! Conner couldn't believe such innocence and allure existed in one woman. Her body and her eyes spoke volumes of her need, her desire. Signals no man would be able to miss. Yet she spoke of inexperience, requesting he show her what to do.

She was every man's dream. A willing woman, sexy as hell, asking to be taught. Goddamn that was hot.

But he had to make sure she really wanted this. After what she'd been through tonight, the last thing he'd do is take advantage of her.

"Are you sure this is what you want?"

Her lips curved into a smile that made his cock jerk against his pants.

"I choose who makes love to me, Conner. And I want you."

He didn't need any more assurances. Gathering her into his arms, he pulled her onto his lap.

God. He'd forgotten she wasn't wearing panties. Just his T-shirt. Her body was warm, inviting, pliable as she relaxed against him and laid her head on his shoulder.

Her hot cunt settled over his jean-clad shaft and he almost came right then. Her moisture soaked through the denim, hot, musky, the scent of her filling the room and signaling her desire.

She felt so damn good in his arms. He wanted to tear the T-shirt off and lick her entire body, putting his scent, his mark all over her. He wanted to come inside her pussy. Deep and hard.

*Don't rush. Katya needs this slow and easy.* He had to rein in his lust. It might kill him, but he'd do it.

Cradling her in his arms like this made him feel protective. And possessive. She trusted him. Considering what she'd been through tonight, that was one amazing gift.

She wanted him to erase Peter's touch from her memories. He'd damn well do that. The only memories he wanted Katya to have were of him. His body on her, in her, taking possession of her.

*Fuck. Too intense. Slow down. Think sex, not mating.*

Maybe this wasn't such a good idea.

She tilted her head back and looked up at him. Her hair was still damp and draped over his arm like black silk. Her eyes were liquid, shimmering in the dim light of the room, dilated with desire. Her lips parted, her tongue swiping over the bottom.

Too late. No way in hell was he going back now.

With a groan he pulled her up and took her mouth, trying desperately to leash his passion. Damn, it was difficult to hold back, especially when she whimpered and wrapped her arm around his neck, sliding her fingers into his hair and pulling him closer. Her passion overwhelmed him. Unexpected, tenuous, yet still fervent as she pressed more fully against his chest, her hip massaging his aching cock.

The taste of her was as intoxicating as the flavor of the brandy that clung to her lips and tongue. He licked her tongue, shuddering at the hot sparks of pleasure that shot between his legs. Rocking his shaft against her hip, he mentally cursed the fact that he still wore clothes. He needed to feel his flesh against hers, needed her wet, steaming hot cunt squeezing his cock.

Concentrating on her pleasure, he skirted his hand over her shoulder and down her arm, loving the buttery soft feel of her skin. Careful not to move too fast, he stroked her hip, kneading her flesh, timing his movements to her reactions. She arched against him, her legs parting as she shifted again.

His cock was going to explode soon if she kept whimpering like that. Her need spurred him on and he lifted the T-shirt, exposing more of her upper thighs and the beautiful treasure between them.

Her mound had a thatch of soft black curls, her pussy lips smooth. The bud of her clit peeked out of its protective hood, begging for his mouth. Moisture glistened along her slit, signaling her readiness for him.

Christ almighty it was hard to hold back.

Katya was lost in a whirlwind of sensations almost too arousing to bear. She'd never felt like this before. So out of control, so desperate for release. Even when she'd released the pressure building inside her with her own hand, she'd never been worked into such a frenzy.

Conner's scent filled her, drove her arousal with his clean, earthy smell. His hard cock pressing against her hip sent her mind into visions of what it would be like to feel him inside her. Tingling sparks of agonizing pleasure thrummed her clit. Her sex poured juices of need between her thighs as her mind conjured up muddled visions of Conner between her legs, touching her, tasting her, fucking her. Her womb quivered just thinking about what it would be like to take his cock in her hands, examine it, run her fingers over the shaft and lick his essence from the tip.

The urge was strong. Too strong to deny this time.

Something in her mind told her to stop, that she was about to make an irrevocable choice, but she pushed it aside, tired of always doing what was right.

If this was wrong, then it was wrong. But it was what she wanted, what she needed.

Desperate for mating, she sat up and turned so that she faced him. She touched every inch of his body, her hands roaming over broad shoulders and muscled arms, settling along his chest. Resting her palm against his heart, she smiled at the racing beat. When he responded with a groan, she investigated further, flicking her fingers over a distended nipple. He sucked in a swift breath. Katya hoped her brandy-soaked mind could commit these sensations to memory.

"I need to feel my skin against yours," he said, his voice rough, intense.

Before she could respond, he lifted the shirt up and over her breasts, tugging it over her head and casting it to the floor.

The way he looked at her was like a shot of pure fire, his gaze burning over every inch of her naked body. She shifted and moved off him, her fingers fumbling over the buttons of his shirt.

Damn brandy. She could barely focus on those tiny little buttons.

Conner brushed her hands aside and quickly unsheathed the buttons, then pulled the shirt off. He stood and reached for the zipper of his jeans. Her gaze targeted his crotch and the outline of his erection pressed against the tight denim.

It looked big. Really big. She swallowed and reached for her glass, taking a long drink of the remaining amber liquid, hoping to moisten her suddenly dry throat.

His fingers poised at the zipper, his gaze raking her body. She could have sworn she saw his cock leap against his jeans.

Slowly, agonizingly slowly, he drew the zipper down, revealing a line of dark, fuzzy hair that disappeared inside the denim. Her next breath shuddered as he pushed the jeans over his hips and slid them to the floor.

His cock sprang up. A wide, mushroom-shaped head led to a thick shaft that made her mouth water. His cock was lined with veins and ridges she wanted to explore with her hands, her mouth. What did he feel like? Hard, soft? The tip looked like velvet. How would it feel inside her?

No, she didn't need another drink this time. She needed to feel that cock buried inside her.

"Keep looking at me like that and my promise to take this slow is going to disappear."

She dragged her gaze away from his cock and to his face. "I don't want to take this slow. I want you inside me, Conner."

The golden green glow of his eyes turned feral, his power evident in the corded muscles of his arms. He reached for her, but despite the fierce draw of his features, was surprisingly gentle. He swooped her into his arms and headed back toward the bedroom.

Blood greeted them. On the sheets, the floor, everywhere.

Visions of Peter's attack came back to her, her anger rising quickly. She felt no fear after what happened, but she was damned pissed off that he had tried to take what she had never offered him.

No. She didn't want to feel anger right now. Not when Conner had stretched her out on a blissful rack of pleasure and anticipation. She pushed thoughts of Peter aside, concentrating instead on the naked man holding her in his arms as if she weighed nothing.

"Shit," he muttered, then pulled the blanket off the floor, tossed it over her and stepped through the French doors leading to her patio.

Cold night air swept across her cheeks. She shivered and Conner pulled her closer, heading swiftly toward his cottage. He pushed the door open and headed straight for his bedroom, depositing her on the coverlet and dragging her blanket away. She scooted up to the pillows and laid back, content to watch the way he moved. Graceful, yet with a barely leashed power she found incredibly erotic. His body was a work of art. She could spend hours just examining the hair sprinkled across his chest and then testing the strength of his broad shoulders.

He was much more than she could have ever expected. There was so much to learn about a man's body. How his skin felt so different than hers, his muscles more pronounced than hers. His scent was unlike anything she'd ever picked up before, and she'd been present during mating rituals, had seen and smelled lupine men.

Nothing could have prepared her for this. Her reaction was different, because Conner was *her* man.

At least tonight.

*Funny the things one thought about when enveloped in a haze of brandy.*

Conner settled on the bed next to her, dragging her onto her side to face him.

"Put your leg over my hip," he commanded.

She lifted her leg and slung it over him, putting her pussy in direct contact with his shaft. Instinctively she rubbed against his cock, dragging her clit against his hard flesh and crying out with the agonizing pleasure.

Conner kissed her, taking her mouth insistently, savagely, no longer holding back as he ravaged her tongue, sucking it between his teeth, sending her spiraling into oblivion. She inched closer and once again rocked her sex against his shaft, moistening it with the flood of her juices.

"Goddamn, Katya. You're so wet." He reached between them, stroking her clit and aligning his cock head between her pussy lips. He teased her, swirling his thumb over the distended bud.

"Oh, God, Conner, I need to come so badly. Please help me." She knew she muttered incoherently, hardly able to put two words together, but she was in desperate need of release. His skin was flame, his mouth an erotic inferno coaxing her response.

"I know exactly what you need, baby," he answered. "Just be patient."

How could she be patient when she wanted him inside her right now?

But he flipped her over onto her back and parted her legs with his knees, placing his palms on either side of her shoulders. He dipped down and dragged his tongue over one nipple. She shrieked and arched her back, feeding him her breast.

He growled and took it greedily, sucking the nipple into his mouth, lapping until she whimpered, begging him to fuck her, to ease the torment raging through her body.

But he didn't. Instead, he tortured the other nipple, sucking, licking, biting it with gentle nibbles. She shook her head from side to side and pleaded for release.

Completion hovered close, her pussy quaking with need, and yet he didn't fuck her! "Dammit, Conner! Please."

"Not yet. I have to make sure you're ready."

How much more ready was she going to get? If he kept tormenting her like this she'd pass out.

Or kill him.

But he slipped down between her legs, his hot breath caressing her thigh.

"Oh, God," she said as she looked down to see him smiling up at her. Unable to tear her gaze away, she watched his tongue flick out and lick the length of her.

Hot, unbridled lightning spiraled through her sex, tremors quaking deep within her belly. He licked again, swirling his tongue in circles around her clit, then covering the bud with his lips and sucking.

She splintered apart, crying out as her climax soared through every part of her, leaving her trembling. Conner held onto her hips and slid his tongue inside her cunt to lap up every drop.

Before she could completely recover, he crawled up and entwined his fingers with hers, lifting her arms over her head and pinning her in place. He took her mouth in a passionate kiss, letting her taste her own cum. It drove her arousal to new heights and she lifted her hips, begging him without words to finish what he'd started.

He loomed over her, his thighs touching hers, his cock head brushing her slit. "Ready?" he asked, his voice tight, his jaw clenched with restraint.

She'd been ready for him since the moment she'd opened the door to her cottage and found him standing there. "Fuck me."

# Chapter Four

🔊

Conner drank in the raw, raging passion in Katya's eyes.

Unfamiliar urges and needs pummeled his senses. He knew, deep down, that he shouldn't be here doing this with her. But the call to mate with Katya was more than he could resist. His body craved the connection with her.

She was willing.

He was more than ready.

Fuck it. Time to stop thinking.

He settled between her legs and she drew her knees up, planting her feet onto the mattress and raising her buttocks, her creamy slit caressing his cock.

Her passion unraveled him. His control slipped. Sliding past her swollen pussy lips, he plunged his cock deep.

She cried out and Conner stilled, realizing he'd just pushed past a barrier that he hadn't expected to be there. Shit! Katya was a virgin!

*Was* a virgin. But not any longer. He'd breached the barrier and buried himself inside her tight sheath. It pulsed around him, trembling, seething like a volcano about to erupt.

"You didn't tell me," he said, kissing the tears that slid along her temple. He was afraid to move.

"Not necessary to tell," she said, speaking through gasps. "I wanted this. Virginity is inconsequential. Quit talking and fuck me."

Once again, she amazed him. And just about killed him as her pussy spasmed around his dick. He moved back and speared her again, this time more slowly, giving her body a chance to adjust.

Slick fluids rushed from her and she wrapped her legs around him, drawing upward, closer, taking his cock as if it had been created just for her cunt. She was a perfect fit for him. Tight, squeezing, drenched with cream. He moved again, mindful of her pleasure as he stroked in and out, scraping that tight little ball inside her pussy.

"Oh, oh, God, Conner, more." She grasped his shoulders, digging her nails into his flesh. He drove harder now, assured that he wouldn't hurt her. Her panting cries and whimpers signaled her pleasure and he wanted her release more than his own.

Grinding his shaft deep inside her, he let it pulse, let that magical spot feel his flesh against it, the hard ridges catapulting her into a keening wail. Her eyes flew open and she met his gaze. Primal lust filled the dark orbs. The human in her receded, the wolf appearing, fierce and hungry. She sucked in her lower lip, her small, even teeth biting down until she drew blood. Her expression tight and determined, she lifted her buttocks, demanding her release.

Her fierce reaction to his strokes had him struggling to keep the wolf at bay. Her eyes glittered and he knew she struggled, too. He wanted to stay human, to ride out this maelstrom of emotion and sensation without losing control. As it was, Katya had already shredded most of the human restraint he had. Her whimpering demands, her urgent pleas for release were his undoing. His balls drew up tight, pulsing with the need to jettison his cum inside her, to mark her in the primal way.

It was time to make her his.

Katya had no idea it would be like this. Fierce, uncontrollable, this desperate urge to relieve the tension coiling tight and hot inside her. Her pussy quaked around Conner's thick shaft, his ridged cock scraping along her sensitive g-spot. Her body spilled copious fluids as she creamed and spasmed over and over again.

And yet these sensations were just a prelude to what was coming. She knew it, he knew it, and it was driving her mad. Release hovered close and no matter how much she tensed and willed it to happen, it teased her, toyed with her, forcing a passion that she wasn't prepared for.

Through the haze of awareness she recognized Conner as the only man to drive these feelings through her body. She knew she'd question that later, as she'd question the choices she made. But right now, the brandy had done its job, giving her tunnel vision. The only thing that mattered was Conner. His skin brushing against hers, his cock powering in and out of her pussy, his mouth covering hers and tasting the blood she'd spilled when she bit her lip.

He tore his lips from her mouth and grazed her neck, reaching underneath to gather her buttocks in his hands, tilting her pelvis upward so he could drive in deeper. She screamed, finally riding the roller coaster of her release. When he bit down on the flesh of her shoulder, her climax hit like a rushing wave, drowning her in sensation she felt deep in her womb.

Conner growled against her, his canines emerging and slicing into her skin. A cry tore from her lips as the sensation served to catapult her into a second orgasm, this time taking him along. He reared back and drove hard, spilling hot jets of fluid inside her.

Even after they'd come he continued to move inside her. Slowly, taking her mouth in a kiss that drove all reason from her mind. His hands moved over her skin, light caresses that lulled her, relaxed her.

Conner rolled off and drew her against his chest, wrapping the blanket over them both.

The last thing she remembered was his lips against her hair as he pressed a tender kiss to her temple. Then she finally gave up, the night, the brandy and the haze of pleasure winning out over her desire to remain awake. She sank into blissful oblivion.

Conner felt Katya finally relaxing against him. When he heard her deep, even breathing, he knew she'd fallen asleep. Too bad he couldn't follow her so easily. Thoughts ran rampant through his mind. Thoughts that demanded examination.

Like what he was going to do now that he'd mated with her. Because despite wanting to think this had just been sex, he knew it had gone much deeper than that. The protective, possessive, wolf part of him demanded that no other man touch her. Ever.

And he sure as hell wasn't ready for that. Not yet, not with her and most definitely not here. This wasn't in the grand plan for him. He was supposed to mate eventually. He'd be assigned to an area by his parents and have to search out a pack and mate there.

They sure as hell hadn't told him it would be Romania. So his gut reaction about Katya had to be wrong. It was probably due to what happened to her tonight with Peter. Since he'd witnessed it and stopped it, he just felt protective toward her. That and the fact she'd just gifted him with her virginity had to be the reason he was so emotional. Because God knew he wasn't typically emotional about fucking.

He wasn't her mate, he was sure of it.

Satisfied that he'd worked out the scenario with logic, he allowed his body to relax. Wrapping his arms tighter around Katya, he inhaled the sweet scent of her skin and closed his eyes, drifting into the darkness.

* * * * *

Katya drifted slowly into consciousness, blinking her eyes and frowning at her dry mouth. She needed water. And a shower, because she was sticky all over.

What the hell had she done last night? She focused on the predawn light sifting in through the French doors, then stilled as realized that she lay next to a strong, warm body.

Heat suffused her skin as she realized who that body belonged to. She shut her eyes, willing what had happened to be nothing but a dream.

But she knew it was real, realized what she had done.

Oh, God, now what?

Conner jerked to a sitting position as a frantic knock and a loud female voice sounded at the front door. He jumped out of bed and quickly shot a look in her direction as if in warning to stay put. Katya heard Elena's voice after Conner opened the door. She followed Conner into the bedroom, a worried look on her face.

"I couldn't find anyone else. Where's Peter? I can't find Katya. Conner, have you—"

Katya sat up in bed just as Elena turned toward her. Her face went pale as she looked over at Conner's naked body and then back to Katya.

"What have you done, cousin?" Elena asked in Romanian.

"Speak English, Elena. It is rude to leave him out of the conversation."

"Are you certain he's going to want to hear what is said?"

Katya glanced at Conner, unable to resist the feminine sigh as she stared at his naked body. Unashamed, he put his hands on his hips and regarded them both with a frown.

"Peter attacked me last night," Katya explained. "Badly."

Elena's eyes widened and she flew to the bed, grasping Katya's hands. "Are you injured?"

"He beat me, tried to rape me, but Conner stepped in before he managed it."

Elena squeezed Katya's hand, then glanced over at Conner, her gaze centered on his crotch. Katya followed Elena's eyes, seeing the dried bloodstained evidence of her former virginity all over Conner's cock.

"You had sex with him," Elena whispered.

"Yes."

"Does he know what this means?"

"Could somebody please tell me what the hell you two are talking about?" he asked.

"Elena, leave us alone, please."

"But I don't think—"

"I'll be fine. I need to talk to Conner alone."

Elena cast a dubious look at Conner, then shrugged. "Scream if you need me. I'll hear you."

After Elena turned and walked out, Conner turned to Katya, one brow arched in a way that had her thinking about wicked hot sex, not telling him the truth.

"Well?"

She swallowed, desperate for a glass of water. Her head felt like a knife had been inserted into her temple and was stuck there. Her mouth was a desert and her pussy was sore. A rather pleasant soreness, though. Despite the ramifications, she didn't regret what happened last night.

But Conner would hate her when he found out.

"I need you to know that I would never have done this under normal circumstances." She hoped he believed her. Entrapment wasn't in her nature. It had to be the trauma, the brandy that had fogged her senses, obliterating her normal common sense. She hadn't waited all these years for the right man just to fall into bed with the wrong one. There was a reason she'd given her virginity so easily to Conner. Unfortunately, even she didn't know what that reason was. How was she supposed to explain it to him?

"Done what?"

"I've remained a virgin all these years for a specific reason."

"And that reason is?"

Taking a deep breath, she said, "I'm the princess of Braslieu, the sole surviving heir to the land and holdings of the Braslieu family and the only remaining royal in the dynasty."

His eyes widened. "You're the princess."

"Yes."

"Why didn't you tell me?"

"Because I don't tell anyone. No one outside those who live in Braslieu knows the identity of the royal family. It's a secret."

He frowned, furrows appearing on his forehead. "Okay, I don't get it. What does that have to do with your virginity?"

This was where it was going to get ugly. She already knew it, but there was no way to prepare him for it. "I remained a virgin because according to custom, the man who takes my virginity is my mate and will rule Braslieu beside me."

For a moment, he didn't move, his facial expression revealing nothing. Then, a slight tic jumped at his temple, his eyes narrowed and he said, "Wanna run that by me again?"

She looked down at her lap, clasping her hands together, feeling horrible because of what she'd done. When she looked at him again, she felt his anger, his confusion, his doubt.

"Last night you mated with the Princess of Braslieu, Conner. We are bound for all eternity now."

The blood drained from Conner's body, leaving a cold, empty chill in its stead.

Mated. Bound. Eternity. He didn't want to hear those words, didn't care for the implication that something occurred that was outside his control, outside his knowledge.

"How could you do that?" he asked, unable to believe that the warm, passionate woman last night could be so deceptive.

"I didn't. Not purposely, anyway. It had to be the brandy, the shock, everything combined together to make me forget that I wasn't supposed to have sex."

He choked out a laugh, reaching for his jeans and sliding them on. He yanked the zipper up and glared at her. "Give me a break, Katya. You didn't remember you were a virgin? You conveniently forgot that having sex meant binding you to the man forever? Do I look that stupid?"

"You don't look stupid at all. I'm sorry, Conner. I didn't mean for this to happen. You have to believe me."

Right now he didn't know what to believe. Could he have been that far off base about Katya? Granted, she had been traumatized last night. No one would set up a scene like the one he'd come upon. No way. It was obvious she wasn't willing to give up her virginity to Peter.

But how could she so easily give it up to him? Peter was her lifelong friend, a Romanian. Whereas Conner was a stranger. And she'd fought Peter until she'd ended up bloodied and bruised because she didn't want to give him her virginity.

Unless... No. No fucking way. No woman was that devious.

Yeah, Conner was a stranger. A rich, connected stranger who could give the Braslieus everything they needed and more. A sanctuary for the wolves. Political connections to battle their government.

God, he *was* stupid.

"Please tell me what you're thinking," she said, her voice a whisper.

He shot a look over at her, his body reacting to the sight of her naked breasts, pink-tipped nipples jutting high and tight, her mouth swollen from his kisses and her hair in sexy disarray around her shoulders.

She was a seductress. The best he'd ever seen.

Because she'd just seduced his free will right out from under him. "I'm thinking you set this whole thing up just to entrap me."

She paled, her eyes wide. "Set you up? How?"

He paced the room, feeling cornered. "After Peter attacked you and I came in, you realized the only way to protect yourself from him, and to secure your family's financial future and the safety of the wolves was to seduce me."

Her frown wasn't the least bit convincing. "You're insane. I would never do anything like that. Conner, I was barely coherent after the attack. And the brandy. I should have never had so much to drink. I didn't know what I was doing."

"You knew exactly what you were doing. I just didn't give you credit for being the conniving bitch you really are. I fell for it. You're good, I'll give you that. But if you think I'm going to lie down and give up my freedom just because you fucked me last night, you're mistaken, princess. I want nothing more to do with you or your family."

Katya forced back the tears, the raw, aching pain lancing her heart like an open wound. Conner's accusations hurt. She understood his anger. She'd have felt the same way if their roles were reversed. But the fact he thought she deliberately gave up her virginity to trap him into bonding with her was ridiculous. And insulting. "Conner, I would never force someone to do what they didn't want to do. Not knowingly, anyway. What happened last night was an accident."

He smirked. "What happened last night was a calculated plan concocted by a coldhearted bitch."

She'd heard enough. She stood, grabbing the discarded blanket from her bed and wrapping it around herself. "I'm not staying to listen to this."

"Good, because I'm not staying either. Find yourself another mate, sweetheart. And while you're at it, another benefactor. Because you won't see a dime from the Devlin Foundation for this venture. You played a high stakes game and gambled your virginity. Too bad it didn't pay off in the big bucks you were looking for."

Right now she hoped to hell he'd leave. Anger suffused her and she was afraid to say any more or linger any longer. "Obviously what you and I experienced last night was completely different, Conner. I did what I did because it seemed natural to do so. Something I've never felt with another man. I thought you felt it, too… That mating frenzy, that feeling of destiny between us. I was wrong. Dead wrong."

She turned and stalked out the door, refusing to stay and see his reaction or listen to him spout more insults about her character. He could go straight to hell. She never wanted to see him again.

As far as her virginity and bonding, she'd have to figure something out. Rules and dynasty be damned. She'd rather be tied up naked and paraded through Bucharest than be mated to Conner Devlin.

# Chapter Five

 හ

Conner paced the cottage, irritated at the smirk on Noah's face. "What the fuck do you find funny about this situation?"

Noah crossed his arms and stretched his legs. "The fact you haven't packed up and left yet. It's been half a day. Plenty of time to arrange for a car to Bucharest. So what's holding you back?"

He wished he knew. Possibly the thought of bursting a blood vessel in mid-flight. Anger made his pulse jet through his veins, the one at his temple throbbing incessantly.

"How could I be so fucking stupid?"

"Seems to come naturally to you," Noah deadpanned.

"Funny." He had absolutely no intention of staying in Romania, no matter what happened with Katya last night. He refused to be forced into a bond that he hadn't chosen.

Maybe he *had* felt mated to her last night, but that was a mistake on his part. He'd gotten his signals confused. His feelings for her had been just some weird aftershock of her trauma. But so much of this debacle didn't make any fucking sense. No way would she have set herself up to be assaulted like that. The thought occurred to him but he'd immediately discarded it. No woman would put herself through that. Besides, he'd seen genuine horror and rage on Katya's face when he'd found Peter on top of her. That kind of extreme emotion couldn't be faked.

He truly believed that after she'd gotten over the situation with Peter, she thought she could entrap him by enticing him into bed. After all, she was gorgeous and it was obvious he was attracted to her.

Then again, why had she run last night outside? Why not stay and let him take her right then?

"Fuck. I'm confused."

"Well, duh."

"Quit helping me, Noah. None of this makes sense. Katya doesn't make sense."

Noah shrugged. "Either you believe her story or you don't. You do have some responsibility here, Conner. You know damn well Mom and Dad aren't going to let you just walk away from this. It was *your* dick in her last night."

Conner whirled on him. "If you'd fucked her, what would you do?"

"I wouldn't have fucked her. I can smell virginity on a woman and I stay far, far away from that trap."

"Yeah, right. You'd have done the same thing I did, given the circumstances. And then you'd be faced with the same dilemma."

"Nah, I'm not as nice as you. As soon as she said she was okay, I'd have hightailed it out of her room. But no, you had to go and play hero. Look where that got you. Next time try my approach—fuck the ones that are experienced. You can tell which ones. Like Elena. Should have chosen her instead. She sure as hell isn't a virgin."

Conner shook his head. Despite Noah's insistence that he was a heartless bastard, Conner knew better. But arguing what ifs with his brother wasn't going to give him the answers he sought. He hadn't seen Katya since she'd stormed out of his room this morning. For all he knew, she'd checked out.

Then again, Noah still had Peter under lock and key, waiting to figure out what the hell to do with him. And Noah had spoken with Elena earlier in the day. So it seemed unlikely that Katya had left.

Right now he needed advice. He put in a call to his parents in Boston and relayed the situation to them. But what he heard in response made his blood boil. Noah listened quietly, arching a brow as Conner argued vehemently with his parents. He couldn't believe what he was hearing!

"What did they say?" Noah asked when Conner ended the call.

"They want me to continue with the project and not do anything to disrupt the political and royal structure of the Carpathians."

"That was it?"

"Dad said if I was going to go around indiscriminately dipping my pen in unknown inkwells, I had to deal with the consequences."

"Christ! Painful metaphor there."

"No shit. That means we stay and I have to commit to being Katya's mate if they're going to force the issue."

"Who are *they*?"

"Hell if I know. I don't even know how their government is set up, or if the Braslieu principality is self-governing. I guess we'll find out when we trek up there."

Noah tilted his head. "You're taking all of this amazingly well."

"I'd like to put a hole through the fucking wall with my fist right now." Frustration boiled inside him, threatening to erupt. What he really wanted to do was call a halt to this entire mess, grab the next plane back to the States and forget he ever met Katya. The prospect of her winning the game of deception she'd so expertly played stuck in his throat like a twenty-pound lobster.

"So where do we start?"

"The last place I want to. We have to go find Katya and figure all this out."

* * * * *

Katya tossed the few things she'd brought along into her small suitcase and gathered up her paperwork. She stopped and stared down at months' worth of preparation and hope, feeling as if she'd let her people down.

She stared at the open front door, feeling out of sorts. The sun was shining on a cool, crisp day. A day to be outside breathing in the fresh air and renewing her spirits.

But that's not how she felt. She felt abysmal, shattered and dark. Despair settled over her like an angry storm cloud, obliterating the bright light outside.

Without the help of the Devlin Foundation, the Carpathian wolves were in danger from hunters and those out to destroy them. The Devlins had been their last hope. And she'd screwed that up.

"I can't believe Conner thought you'd machinate such a devious scheme. What an arrogant ass."

Katya allowed a smile at Elena's diatribe. "I'm not sure I blame him. If the situation were reversed, I might have thought the same thing."

But it wasn't true, and Conner hadn't believed her. He'd said hurtful things to her, crushing her heart. But she couldn't really blame him. By Carpathian law, they were mated now. Not by his choice. And frankly, not by hers, either.

Circumstance had thrown them together. She should have told him last night what would happen if they had sex. If she'd had a clear thought in her head at the time, she would have told him. But her mind had been fuzzy, her emotions scrambled after what happened with Peter. Then she'd consumed way too much brandy. And Conner had been there. A lifeline in a moment of crisis. Warm, comforting, and totally irresistible.

Desire flared and ignited at the memories of what they'd shared last night. She hadn't expected sex to be so overpowering, so all consuming. Once she'd started down that road, the urge to mate had taken over. Still, she should have had the presence of mind to understand the repercussions of her actions. She should have stopped.

"Now what?" Elena asked.

"I have no idea. Clearly Conner isn't going to be agreeable to bonding with me."

Elena's eyes widened. "He has no choice. It is our law."

She nodded and crossed her arms. "But it isn't his law. It's not even Romanian or American law."

"It doesn't matter. He's lupine. There's honor at stake."

That much was true. At least for the Carpathian packs. By mating with her, Conner had forged a life bond as written in the laws of the Braslieu principality. It was legal and binding.

"Yes, it's true. I could force him to marry me."

"Wasn't that what you were intending all along?"

She whirled at the sound of a deep male voice. Conner and Noah stood in the doorway. Her heart lurched, her sex moistening as her body recalled his touch, his scent, the feel of him moving inside her.

Despite what happened, she still wanted him. Rather, her body thought it still wanted him. Her mind and her heart wanted nothing more to do with Conner. She'd only allow herself to be stupid once. "Why are you still here? I would have thought you'd be on a plane back to America by now."

She turned away, refusing to let him see how much he hurt her.

"I'm surprised you didn't have your pack drag me off in chains and toss me in the castle dungeon to await the marriage."

She rolled her eyes, refusing to dignify his idiotic statement with a comment. But she couldn't stand the silence and finally turned around, hands on her hips. "Is there something you want?"

The way his gaze lazily roamed over her body should have angered her. Instead, her pussy quaked and her nipples pebbled. She crossed her arms over her chest to hide the clear outline of the erect buds, but could do nothing to hide the telltale blush that crept up her neck and flamed her face. The corners of his mouth lifted. Damn him, he knew exactly the effect he had on her.

And she'd bet he wasn't the least bit interested in sex right now. He looked at her that way to assert dominance.

Two could play at that game. She stared back, looking him over from the top of his thick black hair, refusing to look away when he pinned her with his sharp blue-green eyes, lingered at his full lips, then traveled slowly down over his broad chest, narrow waist and hips, finally settling at the obvious bulge in his jeans.

Now it was her turn to smirk. She met his eyes and said, "Again, is there something you want?"

"Just trying to figure out what the next step is here."

Was he serious? "You don't really mean to say that you're planning to stay, to honor the mate bond between us."

"That's not what I said at all. Only that it bears…further investigation."

She wanted to know why he'd had a change of heart. Or was it even his change of heart? He looked irritated, that vein near his temple pulsing rapidly. Whatever happened wasn't his doing. Yet he was still here, and for some reason she wasn't unhappy about that. "We're heading back to the castle today."

"You'll need escort. I have Peter locked up in my room and I assume you'll want to take him with you," Noah said. "Of course, if you'd rather leave him behind, I'd be more than willing to…dispose of him."

Peter. She'd conveniently obliterated thoughts of him from her mind. But he was a Braslieu problem, not a Devlin one. She shuddered at the thought of exactly what Noah would do to Peter. Not that he didn't deserve it, but some things were best left to Braslieu laws. "Yes, we'll be taking him with us."

"Then we're going with you," Conner said, his tone brooking no argument.

She started to object, then shrugged. She and Elena couldn't possibly escort Peter up the mountain alone, and she didn't trust anyone outside the castle to come along as security. So that left the only two people who knew what happened, who knew what they were.

"We leave in an hour."

Conner nodded and left, Noah following.

Katya exhaled and slipped into the chair next to the desk to calm her raging heartbeat.

"You two are bonded. Destined," Elena said. "I can feel it surrounding both of you. Hell, cousin, I can smell it on both of you. The mating frenzy is so obvious I'm surprised the two of you hadn't realized it last night."

That was the problem. She hadn't realized much of anything last night. But Conner, her destiny? Highly unlikely.

This was a mess. How they were going to resolve it was an unknown, but somehow, someway they'd have to.

She was a princess compromised. Something would have to be done about that. What that something was, she had no idea.

* * * * *

They had to take two vehicles. The small rough terrain vehicles couldn't carry all five of them plus luggage.

Elena and Katya traveled in the lead vehicle with the luggage, while Conner and Noah escorted Peter, who wasn't very happy to have his wrists tied to the door handle.

"I resent this treatment," he muttered.

Conner turned around to look at Peter, hanging onto the roll bar as they hit a particularly large boulder in the road. "I'll bet Katya resented your treatment of her last night, too."

It was all he could do not to beat the shit out of the bastard. From the faint bruises on his face and the swelling that hadn't quite gone down, Noah must have worked him over after he'd dragged Peter from Katya's bedroom last night.

"Katya is *my* woman. She understands how things are between mates. You have no right to interfere."

Tension seethed, dangerous rage boiling just underneath his skin. Conner turned around, determined to ignore Peter until they reached the castle. He swore that if they didn't mete out some type of adequate justice, he'd just have to take matters into his own hands. That bastard needed to pay for what he'd done to Katya.

"She is already mated to me. I will kill you if you come anywhere near her."

Conner shook his head at Peter's comment, not bothering to correct the man's misassumption. Obviously he took the two of them for fools. And he didn't know that Conner had mated with Katya.

"She likes it rough. That's all you saw that night. You interfered needlessly. My Katya prefers to be tied up and forced to have sex. It's the only way she can come."

"You fucking prick." That was it. Conner unbuckled his seat belt, intending to climb into the backseat and beat Peter into a lifeless pulp.

Noah stopped him by laying a hand on his arm. "He's digging his own grave. Let him be. One way or another, he'll be taken care of."

Surprised Noah wasn't encouraging him to kill the bastard, Conner shrugged and rebuckled his belt, conjuring up ways to torture Peter. Painful, bloody ways. He'd bet he could get the wimp to cry like a little girl, too. He'd love to show him what it felt like to be helpless and at the mercy of someone bigger, stronger and meaner.

The vehicle in front lurched to a stop at the top of a rise, then inched forward slowly. When they pulled up alongside Katya's vehicle, Conner pulled off his shades and climbed out of the vehicle to stare at the sight in front of them.

71

Like a beacon revealing a lush paradise, the sun had broken through the dense clouds overhead, shooting spectacular rays of light over the valley floor. The valley was an emerald oasis of thick grass, filled with wildflowers of every color that seemed to grow in clumps like bouquets.

High above the clearing, forbidden and imposing, stood a tall castle of grey stone, so light it was almost white. Crumbling and in disrepair, it had to be centuries old with two towers reaching toward the sunlight as if beckoning the renewing warmth. Iron gates surrounded the area in front of them, with tall fencing as far as he could see.

Those fences would never hold in a wolf that didn't want to be contained. He'd have to think about how to fix that.

Woodland surrounded the castle, thick and pungent with the smell of fresh earth and pine. Conner heard but couldn't see water flowing somewhere around them. Mountain springs must flow throughout the castle grounds. The tops of the trees reached almost the to the highest point of the castle towers, sheltering it to the sides, yet the castle front stood unfettered by foliage or camouflage of any kind.

Katya turned to them, a glow of pride on her face. "Welcome to Braslieu Castle."

Her words were spoken with all the dignity befitting royalty, her eyes sparkling with a glow of excitement. Katya hopped out of the vehicle and approached the gated entrance, speaking in rapid Romanian to the guards stationed there.

He really needed to learn their language, since it would have been good to know what she said to the guard. The sentry nodded, eyed him and Noah suspiciously, then opened the gates and let them through.

Noah shot Conner a look that said "be on watch". They really had no idea what to expect.

They drove up a long, narrow road toward the front of the castle. Thick bushes lined both sides, obscuring their view of the surroundings. They parked their vehicles at the front entrance. Two men came out and Katya directed them toward Peter. The men frowned, their faces red with anger as they hurried toward Peter.

Conner grinned, saluted a now very pale Peter a goodbye, and followed Katya and Elena in.

They stepped into a foyer that had seen better days, yet still maintained an old-world charm that Conner found pleasing.

Though the wood floors needed resurfacing, they were still beautiful, no doubt made from the trees surrounding the castle. The curving staircase off the foyer was carpeted with an old, threadbare pile. The same kind of wear showed on the tapestries decorating the wall. Faded beauty surrounded him. This place needed a major overhaul, yet it still shined clean and with the pride of the people who cared for it.

The two men dragged Peter inside. Before long, a crowd gathered, whispering to each other and eyeing both he and Noah, along with Peter. Katya spoke to the guard who started to drag Peter away, but he dug in his heels and shouted something in Romanian that made the crowd gasp and all heads turn toward the princess.

Katya shook her head, wide-eyed, speaking in short, clipped sentences. Goddamit, what the fuck was happening? He couldn't understand a word, but whatever Peter had said caused quite a commotion.

Noah brought Elena over. "Translate," he commanded.

She nodded and said, "Peter just announced that he and Katya were mated."

Christ! He really should have killed that prick. He started forward, but Elena said, "Don't. They don't even know who you are. You won't be welcome if you interfere."

He goddamned would interfere. That sonofabitch was still trying to stake his claim on Katya.

"She denies it," Elena explained. "But Peter insists they are mated and therefore must marry. He claims to have had sex with her in the cottage."

"But she just denied it, right?"

Elena shot a worried glance toward Conner. "It's his word against hers. And if the doctors examine her, they will agree she is no longer a virgin. It's custom to do regular inspections of the princess. Saves embarrassment later should a mate be found, only to discover his bride is not the virgin she claimed to be."

Conner glanced toward Katya, who refused to look in his direction. Instead, she held her chin up and didn't say a word. She wasn't going to deny Peter's claim!

"Why isn't she saying anything?" he asked Elena.

Noah answered, instead. "She's giving you your way out, you moron."

Conner's gaze shot to Peter, who stood smugly and triumphantly at Katya's side. No way. No fucking way! He couldn't allow Katya to be mated to that bastard.

Whether he liked it or not, whether it was planned or happened by circumstances, Katya was his woman. The thought of another man's hands on her sent a painful shot to his gut.

"Goddamit." He strode through the crowd, oblivious to the whispers in Romanian. Katya shot him a wide-eyed look and shook her head as if to warn him off. He ignored her silent plea, stepped beside her and slid his hand in hers. "This is what you wanted, babe. Like it or not, I'm all yours."

Elena hurried beside him, obviously intending to translate.

He turned to the crowd and said, "Peter lies. He tried to rape your princess. He beat her violently." He waited for Elena to translate and until the gasps and murmurs died down. Then he looked over at Peter, who'd paled significantly.

"She is mine!" Elena translated Peter's words, but Conner shot him a smirk and said, "No, she is mine. Katya and I mated last night. The bloodstained evidence is on the sheets of my cottage."

A collective gasp went up, then shouts came from the crowd. They threw their hands up in the air, confusion written on their faces. Conner looked at Katya who looked white as a ghost. "Corroborate."

She looked up at him, shook her head, then back at the crowd, speaking so quietly it was difficult to hear.

Elena leaned over and whispered in his ear. "Katya, Princess of Braslieu, has just claimed Conner Devlin as her life mate. Congratulations, Conner. You're engaged."

# Chapter Six

All hell broke loose after Katya admitted that everything Conner had said was true. The crowd cheered, so he obviously wasn't unwelcome. What followed was a blur of congratulations spoken in Romanian by hundreds of strangers. They shook his hand, kissed his cheeks, clapped him on the back and toasted with champagne.

Peter, on the other hand, was furious. He said Conner and Katya were lying, but by the time Noah corroborated the claim and Elena relayed what she knew of the event, no one believed him. Katya still bore enough of the faint wounds of his attack that it was easy to see she hadn't made up the story.

After realizing that Peter had, in fact, attacked the princess, an emergency meeting of the council took place. It was behind closed doors and Conner wasn't invited, but Elena filled him in on the results.

Peter had been banished from the pack, from the castle, and from the Braslieu lands. Since he had no surviving family, he was cast out alone with only his personal belongings. Furious, he screamed at them, vowing revenge on Conner and Katya both.

Whatever. If they hadn't gotten rid of him, Conner would have arranged for his disposal. Peter was a threat to Katya and that he'd never allow.

Some of this still didn't make sense. If Katya was after his money and had tried to trap him into marriage, why would she stand there silently while Peter claimed her?

Of course. She knew after last night that there was no way Conner would ever let Peter lay a hand on her again. She'd counted on his honor and once again he'd played right into her scheme. She was one sharp woman. He'd bet her people knew very little of Katya's intent to use him and his family's money to pour money into protecting the wolves.

Though she didn't have to trap him into marriage to get it. If their need had been valid, the Devlin Foundation would have been more than happy to provide the funding. So what was her scheme?

Judging from the poor condition of the castle, it was obvious she wanted much more than just a refuge for the wolves. That was her plan. She didn't just want some of his money. She wanted it all.

Fuck it. He'd made the choice to stay on and it was too late to back out now. But this game wasn't going to be played her way. Oh, no. Conner had his own plan for running things. Mating with Katya made him prime alpha of the pack.

The prime alpha ran the pack and all the holdings. His way.

Katya would find that she'd bitten off way more than she could chew. And the best place to start would be right here, right now.

Now that the commotion of the day had passed, the crowds dispersed, leaving only Elena, Noah and Katya in the great room. Katya still hadn't made eye contact with him, in fact seemed to be avoiding him completely.

She could try. But he had plans for his new…fiancée.

"We going to stand here all day or can we get unpacked?" Noah asked.

Conner grinned. Great way to start.

Katya nodded and motioned to one of the men standing in the doorway. "I'll arrange to have your luggage brought up to your rooms."

Conner said, "Arrange to have my luggage taken to your room."

Her eyes widened, then narrowed. "I don't think so."

"Oh, I do think so, princess. We're mated. We've bonded. That means I sleep with you. Tonight, tomorrow night and every night after that."

She blanched, her gaze darting to Elena, who shrugged and stated, "He has the right as your life mate to sleep anywhere he pleases, including with you."

"Damn," she muttered, more to herself than to anyone else. She looked up and nodded. "Very well. If that's what you want."

"Oh, I want a lot more than that, princess." She'd find out soon enough exactly what he wanted. And how often. She may have played her game well enough to trap him, but he didn't behave well in a cage. Katya would find her pet wolf had sharp teeth, jagged claws and a fierce bite.

She cast him a wary glance and led them up the stairs, asking Elena to show Noah to his room. Elena's eyes glimmered with lust and Noah offered a lazy smile as he shut the door behind them. Katya continued down the long hallway, opening the double doors to the room at the end.

Late afternoon sunlight streamed in through floor-to-ceiling windows covered only by sheer drapes. The floors were wood, hidden by the occasional ornamental rug, showing the same signs of wear as the carpeting outside the room.

The bed was a magnificent, king-sized four-poster. A shorter person would need a stool to climb on top of the thick mattress. A golden coverlet in satin made the bed the focal point of the room.

The rest consisted of seating areas, sofas, a small library and another door leading to the bathroom.

Plenty of space for both of them. And the big bed had his mind straying to thoughts of sex. He may hate Katya for what she'd done to him, but he still wanted her with a primal lust that shook him. He adjusted his tight jeans, his mind already planning the evening's activities.

"It's almost time for dinner. I'll allow you to unpack. We meet in the dining room at seven."

She started to walk out but he grabbed her by the upper arm. She glared at him, trying to tug free, but he held her in place.

God, she smelled good. Like wildflowers and an underlying scent of sex that drifted into his senses and hardened him completely.

Her eyes widened. "Let go of me, Conner."

"Not a chance, princess. You had your chance to let me go last night. Now I'm never letting you go. I'm your alpha now. Your mate. You do what I say."

When she didn't respond, he added, "Whatever I say. Whenever I say it. However I want it. You're mine. Don't ever forget that."

He loosened his hold on her arm and she jerked away from his grasp. "Like I said. Dinner is at seven. You miss it, you fend for yourself." She shut the door behind her and Conner turned toward his luggage, feeling much more in control of his destiny now than he'd felt after finding out he'd mated the princess.

This was going to be fun.

* * * * *

Katya paced the kitchens, ignoring the curious stares of the people putting the evening meal together.

Living under the same roof with Conner was going to be torment. How would she manage to keep her aloof distance while craving him with a hunger that left her breathless?

She was supposed to be furious with him for treating her like a conniving con artist, not lusting after him and hoping he'd throw her down on the nearest floor and fuck her the same way he had yesterday. Even his commands to her before she left the bedroom made her wet with anticipation. His claiming dominance over her, his not-so-subtle innuendos about her giving him exactly what he wanted. Part of her was enraged at this arrogance. The other part of her thrilled at the sensual promise in his words.

It had to be lupine mating frenzy. There was no other explanation for it. She'd had a taste of her mate and it wasn't nearly enough to satisfy her. Wolves mating for the first time were known to go for weeks having nonstop sex, until the crazed lust was satisfied. She'd only had a glimpse of what it was like to mate with Conner.

She hated how he felt about her, but she needed him inside her.

The sounds of people gathering in the dining room signaled it was time for her to go into dinner. She prayed for the strength to make it through without any altercations. Despite the fact Conner didn't want to be prime alpha of the pack, he'd accepted the position. Now it was time for him to show whether he could lead her people or not.

He and Noah were already present and seated when she walked through the door. He'd taken her normal place at the head of the table, deliberately no doubt. His arched brow indicated he was prepared for her to battle him on this point. He was baiting her.

Katya wasn't stupid. She knew to choose her battles wisely. A chair in the dining room wasn't worth a ruckus. Besides, it was important her people accept him as the wolf who would rule beside her. If she didn't accept him, they never would. Putting her personal feelings aside for the good of the pack, she sat next to him and across from Noah.

Her people relaxed and began to eat. Conversation was kept at a minimum, especially considering Conner and Noah didn't speak their language. While many of them had a good command of English, some didn't. Interpreting was necessary throughout the meal.

Elena began to teach Conner and Noah a few words and phrases in Romanian. They seemed eager to learn and adept at picking up the language.

"I'd like to begin daily lessons in your language, starting tomorrow," Conner said to Elena.

She nodded and said, "Of course. I am available whenever you are ready to begin."

It irked her that her cousin didn't even look over at her for approval. While Conner would rule by her side, Katya didn't want everyone to think he'd taken over her duties. He would be her mate, but didn't possess royal blood. She was the sole Braslieu royal survivor, and as such occupied the prime alpha spot in the pack. She made a mental note to speak with Elena about this tomorrow.

Conner ignored her throughout dinner. At least verbally. But he glanced her way often, his gaze hot, intense, searing through her cool reserve. A clear challenge to her ability to remain impervious to him.

He had much to learn. She was a Braslieu. Made of strong Romanian and Carpathian stock. She could handle whatever game he played with her. If he thought her a coldhearted bitch now, she'd show him exactly how frigid she could be. Her ridiculous lupine mating hormones be damned.

When dinner was over, she stood, intending to hide out somewhere. Anywhere but wherever Conner was. She turned to walk out.

"Katya."

She stopped at the sound of Conner's voice, turning and offering an icy smile. "Yes?"

"I'd like to spend the evening alone with you in the house."

Not a chance. "Other people live in this house, Conner. Not possible."

Elena said, "I'm sure we could arrange some alone time for the two of you. Nice night for a run outside in the woods, anyway."

She cast a glare at her cousin, who smiled and shrugged, then hurried from the room, stating she'd alert the rest of the household to vacate for the evening.

"Your people think you are desperate to be alone with me."

He walked toward her. She skirted around him and smoothed the tablecloth along the table. "My people are misinformed."

"We're mated now, Katya. You wanted me last night. I assume that hasn't changed."

The egotism of the man! She turned and stormed toward him. "You assume wrong. Everyone assumes wrong. After accusing me of deliberately trapping you into a marriage you don't want, do you really believe I'd be interested in having anything to do with you?"

"I think you're more than interested," he said, stepping forward to lift a lock of hair from her shoulder. "You want me."

Her breath stuttered but she reached up and yanked her hair from his grasp. "I don't want you."

"I can smell you, Katya. Your pussy juice smells like nectar to me. You make that scent just for me."

He lied. He couldn't smell anything, despite the fact her panties were wet and her breasts felt swollen and achy. Ignoring the wants of her body, she threw her shoulders back. "Let me make this perfectly clear, Conner. I will never want you. What happened between us was a mistake. I gave you the chance to back out, but you chose to acknowledge we had mated. That means we're stuck with each other, like it or not."

"Oh, I like it just fine." Undaunted, he stepped toward her and ran his knuckles across her cheek.

Fire blazed a trail after his touch, her body quaking with the need to touch him, taste him, beg him to do what he'd done to her last night. But she was stronger than her needs. Her pride would never allow acquiescence to him. "Don't touch me."

He arched a brow. "Are you certain? Your choice, of course, but I can make you want me."

She laughed at him. "No, Conner. You can't."

"Is that a challenge?"

*Don't do it. Don't say the words. This game is stupid and you're playing right into his hands.* But damn if she was just as eager to show him she could withstand his charm as he was to prove her wrong. "Give it your best shot."

Conner's lips curled in a smile, anticipation filling him with desire for the Romanian beauty.

He'd never found innocence particularly attractive. But seeing it reflected in the wary eyes of the woman before him, it aroused him more than he ever thought possible.

He was struck by the sheer liquid softness of her skin. Her lips parted and she breathed heavily, her breasts rising against her sweater, outlining their shape and the rigid nipples he recalled so clearly.

"Relax," he whispered, taking a step closer and cupping the nape of her neck to draw her toward him.

Her body tensed and she stiffened.

"Calm down, Katya. This won't hurt a bit."

He almost saw her lips curl into a smile. Almost. She still stood like a stone statue, rigid and immobile.

Frankly, her acceptance of his challenge surprised him. And aroused him. Tiptoeing around her wasn't going to ease the tension. Desire wavered between them like an impenetrable wall—a wall they both wanted down but neither would make the first move.

He might not be happy about the situation she'd forced him into, but he'd be damned if he'd leave her untouched. Katya was his mate now and he wanted to fuck his woman. Deciding the best way was to knock the wall down was simply to plunge right in, he pulled her close and covered her lips with his.

Absorbing her gasp by fitting his mouth over hers, he slid his tongue inside and tasted her unique flavor. Warm, spicy, like brandy. Sensuous, full bodied and rich, like the lush woman under his hands.

He reached around and ran his hands up and down her spine, gently pressing in at the small of her back and forcing her hips forward.

Her sex brushed his rapidly growing hard-on and he inhaled sharply.

She tensed again, and he pulled back. "This would be a lot easier if you relaxed a bit."

Defiance sparked in her eyes. "I'm not going to make it easy for you."

He knew the challenge wasn't the only reason for her tension. Like him, she didn't like giving in. She was as alpha as he. That's why they made a good match.

Hell, what was he saying? He didn't want this match any more than she did. So why was he here, his cock hard as steel and twitching to slide inside her heat?

Besides, he liked her this way. A little spunk, a little fire. The last thing he wanted was a pliant rag doll in his arms. No, his tastes ran more toward the wild and untamed. He'd wager she was full of pent-up sexuality just dying for the right man to let it loose.

He was one lucky man. Now he needed to be a shrewd one, because if he lost this battle of wills with her, he'd lose the respect of the pack.

He reached behind her and pulled the clasp holding her hair up, letting it spill over her shoulders. Dark as midnight and soft as her skin, it floated over his fingertips as he threaded his hand through the mass of curls.

"You're beautiful," he said, dipping down to steal a taste of her lips. He rimmed her bottom lip with his tongue, coaxing entrance into the heated recesses of her mouth. Her body trembled and she tensed as if she'd fight back, but he refused to yield, licking at her teeth, sliding his lips over hers until, with a sigh, she opened her mouth, tangling her tongue with his.

Remembering to keep her relaxed, he massaged her back again in slow circles, starting at her mid-spine and working his way down. When he splayed his hands over her buttocks and drew her against his erection, she moaned, a clear signal that she was responding without thinking.

Exactly the way he wanted her.

Conner pulled away from her delectable mouth and pressed his lips against her jawline, moving downward over her throat with his tongue. She tasted earthy, elemental, arousing. He glanced through the open drapes at the partial moon, the beast within him raging to be free.

That would come soon enough. Now he had more important matters to attend to.

The effort it took to keep his impulses at bay was great. So great, in fact, that Katya had to feel the tightly coiled tension in his muscles. Then again, she wasn't touching him at all. She might have yielded her mouth, but her body had yet to follow suit.

He'd remedy that soon enough. No way was he going to feel like he'd been strung on a rack of torturous sensation without dragging her along with him.

The war raging within him consumed his every thought. The desire to take, to overpower, the natural inclination and urges of the part of him that was lupine wanted to take over. The human part of him put on the brakes, reminded him what

Katya had endured recently, and wanted no comparison between him and Peter. He'd go slow until she was ready.

Not that she'd ever admit to being ready. But he'd know when she was.

*Lesson one. Command.*

He leaned back and searched her face. Her flushed cheeks and panting breaths told him what she refused to voice. She may not react, but she felt.

"Touch me, Katya."

She shook her head. "No."

"Afraid you'll find you like it too much? Afraid you'll lose the challenge?"

"I don't have to respond. You have to do the taking. I am to just...stand here."

His lips curled. "That's not what you want."

She arched a brow. "Do not presume to know what I want, Conner."

Just as he expected, she wasn't going to give in easily. But he so loved a challenge.

"Tell me," he said, sliding his fingers just under the hem of her sweater. "Do you feel this?"

When he made contact with the bare skin of her belly, she flinched, her abdominal muscles tightening. The pupils of her eyes dilated when he skimmed the waistband of her pants.

"Do you?"

"Do I what?"

"Feel it."

"Of course."

She tried to act nonchalant, but her body reacted.

"How about this?" He reached inside her sweater with both hands, the warmth of her skin igniting his passions. Moving steadily upward, he skimmed her rib cage, resting his hands just under her breasts.

Her breath labored and she shuddered with each inhalation. His fingers were only inches from her nipples.

She didn't say a word.

Neither did he. Instead, he showed her with his hands what he could give her if she'd only ask. He stepped behind her, pulling the sweater up and over her head.

Reaching underneath the mass of dark curls, he swept them over her shoulders to bare her back to him. Sliding his hands upward, he massaged the nape of her neck, pressing close enough to nestle his crotch against her buttocks. Her heat surrounded him, making him desperate to get on with it. He fought for control but he could so easily lose it with her. She tempted him too much.

She tried to mask it, but he heard the whimper. Conner leaned in, whispering in her ear.

"When I fuck you from behind, I'll grab your neck between my teeth and hold you in place. You're mine, Katya. And because of that, I'll possess you completely."

She didn't speak, but her body quivered.

So far, so good.

*Lesson two. Relentless pursuit.*

Keeping his fingertips light and easy, he stroked her shoulders, down her arms, kissing her neck while he explored her upper body with his hands. When he reached around and cupped her breasts, she froze.

Not from fear, though.

Anticipation. Need. Raging desire. Thank God what he felt wasn't one-sided. Despite her cool reception, Katya wanted this. If her damn pride didn't stand in her way, he knew she'd be willing, even eager.

Fighting for patience, he continued his exploration of her body. Swirling his thumbs over the globes, he inched closer to her nipples. He peeked over her shoulder to see the erect buds, poised and ready for his touch.

But he wanted to take this slow. Torment her a little, make her want it so badly she'd forget all about the stupid fucking challenge and just beg him to take her. The only way to ensure that would happen would be to surprise her. She'd expect him to want it fast. He wasn't going to take it fast.

So instead of running his fingers over her nipples, he skated the line of her ribs again, grasping her waist and pulling her gently against his erection.

"You make me hard, Katya. Your body, your scent, the little sounds you make. You think I can't feel your reactions? Can you feel mine?" He moved against her again, but she didn't respond.

He closed his eyes and inhaled the musk of her arousal, rocking his hard-on back and forth against her buttocks. He set a rhythm, and soon enough she was inching back toward him.

Toward his cock, as if she searched for it, needed it.

And it was damn well ready for her, too.

But not yet. In order to torment her, he'd have to suffer the same torture.

Waiting.

He was going to die of acute arousal before this was over.

"Your skin melts under my hands," he murmured, sliding his fingers inside the waistband of her pants again, moving just far enough to touch soft, heated skin. When he moved one hand to the front near her zipper, she backed against his cock again as if she was trying to escape his probing fingers.

But there was no place she could hide from him. He had her in front, and he had her in back.

Soon, he reminded himself. Be patient.

But his patience was quickly wearing thin.

And judging from the harsh rasps of her breath, hers was, too.

"Do you want me?" he asked.

It took her a moment to reply. "No."

She wasn't a very good liar. "Maybe I haven't been thorough enough in my efforts."

He moved in front of her and searched her face. Desire etched frown lines on her forehead, the darkening honey color of her eyes glowed with a primal lust he recognized all too well, and the way she swiped her tongue across her parched lips was a silent signal of wanting.

"Thirsty?"

She nodded.

He led her into the kitchen and opened a bottle, pouring a glass of brandy. She held out her hand to take it from him. But he pulled back. "You need something, I'll give it to you. Drink."

She sighed, her frustration evident, but opened her mouth dutifully while he held the glass to her lips.

Watching her sip the golden liquid made his balls tighten. The way she licked the rim of her glass, then her own lips, made him want to see the same kind of reaction when he came in her mouth. He wanted her to take his cum the way she took the brandy. Eagerly, thoroughly, swallowing every drop and then licking her lips for any leftover flavor.

Resisting the urge to stroke his cock, he took a couple long swallows of the fiery liquid, enjoying the slow burn of his belly as the brandy warmed its way down.

Then he leaned in, tasting the sweet liquor on Katya's lips, once again thrusting his tongue inside her mouth to swirl their flavors together. Tongue to tongue, lips to lips, he fit his mouth over hers as if to show her how well they meshed.

Soon, he'd show her much more than his mouth.

Taking a step back, he admired the swell of her breasts, the thrusting nipples that begged for his touch, his mouth. Waiting to touch and taste her was agony. His balls were twisted in a vise of tight need that threatened to send him to his knees.

Instead, he pressed his lips against her neck, lingering at the pulse point there and counting each rapidly thrumming beat.

Her racing blood told him exactly what he needed to know.

*Lesson three. Move in for the kill.*

He reached for her breasts, cupping them once again, feeling their weight as they settled into his palms. Then he swirled his thumbs around the areolas, circling them over and over until her nipples pebbled to sharp points.

He looked up and met her gaze, willing her to tell him she wanted him to touch them, lick them.

But she remained mute. He'd really love to know how she'd react if there wasn't a challenge between them.

His thumbs flicked the buds. She gasped and her musky scent grew stronger. When he bent down and covered one crest with his lips, teasing the swollen nub with his tongue, she couldn't hide her moan. He did the same with the other, then alternated back and forth, each time feeling the nipples tighten, her breasts grow warmer. Katya could barely hold her whimpers now.

She was weakening.

And he was already destroyed.

When he looked up at her again, the fierce arousal on her face set him on fire. He reined in the beast just as the thick hairs began to pop out on his arms.

It wasn't yet time to become the wolf.

"Are your panties wet?"

She didn't answer.

"I guess I'll find out for myself, then."

Before she could utter an objection, he moved to her jeans and popped the button open, sliding the zipper down and reaching for the waistband, pushing the denim over her hips. Her skin burned, singeing his fingers as he moved lower.

"Wait!" she said.

He stopped.

But she didn't say anything.

"What is it?" Although he already knew the answer. She was quickly losing control, and she wanted him to stop.

"Katya, is there something you want to say?"

In a matter of minutes, this would be over.

Thank God. Because if he didn't get her to give in soon, he'd be the one begging. Or he'd turn and simply take her in the primal mating of the wolf. But that's not the way he wanted to do this tonight. Tonight, he'd take her as a human.

If he could keep the beast within him locked up long enough to see it through.

# Chapter Seven

ɮ

Katya was unable to speak.

What was she going to say? Stop? If she stopped him, he'd win. If she didn't stop him, he'd win. Why had she agreed to this stupid challenge, anyway? As it was she could barely hang onto whatever shred of rational thought remained. If he undressed her completely, if he saw the moist evidence of what he was doing to her, if he took her up one more torturous step, she'd burst and beg him to fuck her.

Then where would she be? Under his control, under his rule.

Never! She hadn't worked this hard for so long, alone, to give it up to the first upstart foreigner who decided he could do it better.

"Katya," The way he said her name made her shiver. It poured off his lips like sweet, dark brandy, smooth and sensual and warming her from the inside out.

She looked up at him.

Heavens, he was beautiful, his eyes dark with desire, his hair falling over his face in a way that made her want to reach out and sweep it back. His cock was like steel as it brushed against her aching sex.

"Katya. Tell me what you want."

"Nothing. You may continue," she finally said, mentally preparing herself for what was to come. She'd endure it, with no response. She wasn't going to give in. She'd steel herself not to feel, not to react, no matter what he did to her. Then later, she'd massage away the blistering ache of arousal by fucking herself with her own hand, masking her screams into her pillow.

Returning to his task, Conner pulled the thin strings at her hips, dragged her panties down over her legs and cast them aside.

But instead of standing, he remained kneeling in front of her, his mouth in perfect alignment to her throbbing sex.

"You're wet," he whispered, reaching out and swiping his finger against the swollen folds of her slit.

She jerked and trembled, so close to orgasm that the barest touch of his fingers inflamed her nearly over the edge.

But if she came, he'd have her.

She fought it, trying to think horrible thoughts. Her parents' death, what happened with Peter, and now being mated to Conner. She forced her mind into pain, into loss, into need.

But need won out, reminding her that she had been alone too long, that the lupine within her craved a mate, a companion, a father for the children she was desperate to bear.

Her body was so primed, so ready, that she had to bite down on her lip to keep from blurting out the words Conner wanted to hear.

She was jerked back to reality by the feel of something hot and wet against her clit. She opened her eyes and saw Conner's head buried between her legs, his tongue snaking out and tasting her wet cunt.

He barely touched her with the lightest of strokes, yet devastated her with sensation.

She'd dreamed of a man licking between her legs, tasting the copious juices that poured forth from her aroused sex. Conner gave her all that she'd dreamed of and more. She wanted to die, to scream, to come. She wanted to beg Conner not to stop until he drove her over the edge.

In an effort to get away from the sensations that pummeled her, she backed against the counter, the sharp edge of the tile digging into her back. Raising up on her tiptoes, she tried anything she could to skirt the devil's tongue swiping back and forth against her throbbing clit.

But she couldn't escape. From the man or the sensations.

Mercifully, he pulled away and stood. Her body and her mind warred. She was glad for the respite, but her body screamed at Conner to damn well finish what he'd started.

Maybe he'd given up, convinced she'd never come. That wasn't so bad. She still balanced precariously on the edge of orgasm, but she'd take care of that problem herself.

Her sigh of relief was mixed with trembling arousal that wouldn't abate. She fought the urges. If she just held on a few more minutes, she'd get the release she so desperately needed. She just had to get dressed and rush upstairs to caress herself to a blistering orgasm.

But before she could offer a smug smile of triumph, Conner lifted her into his arms.

"What are you doing?!"

He didn't answer, just walked across the kitchen and laid her on the oak table, pushing her shoulders back so she was flat on the surface.

When she moved to sit up, his strong hand kept her pinned.

"You mean we're not done?"

Conner arched a brow. "Not by a long shot, baby. I've been eyeing this table since I walked into the room."

He pulled up a chair, spread her legs, and situated himself between them, his mouth lowering toward her sex again.

Oh, God. This wasn't good at all. Now he sat comfortably at the table between her legs, looking like a man about to enjoy a feast.

Only he was feasting on her cunt.

Conner went to work on her, earnestly sucking and nibbling at her clit, then traveled down to lap up the juices pouring onto the tabletop. He licked the length of her, sliding his tongue inside her pussy to fuck her with its soft tip, then moved again to her clit.

Surely not every male in the world was as talented with his mouth as Conner Devlin. He had such an unfair advantage. A gloriously handsome man faced with a woman who loved sex, loved touching herself, enjoyed daily orgasms, and whose body was desperately ready to mate.

She felt the tremors and knew damn well Conner had, too. He quickened his movements, alternating thrusting his tongue inside her pussy and swirling it over her painfully erect clit.

He was driving her toward an orgasm she didn't have a chance in hell of holding back. How could she have ever hoped to win this battle?

She was about to give up all her power, all her control, everything she had built since her parents died. For what?

For a climax?

But she knew she'd already lost. For that matter, she'd lost the first time she'd laid eyes on Conner and the wolf within her had identified a need to mate with him. She may not like it, but if there was one thing she recognized, it was when to admit defeat.

\* \* \* \* \*

Conner knew the moment Katya had given up control. Hell, he gave her credit for lasting this long. Not that he was the best lover in the world, but he tuned into her body's signals right from the start and she'd been primed and ready to shoot off like a rocket before he'd ever touched her pussy.

Her fingers let go of their death grip on the edge of the table and she spread her legs wider, easing the tension in her body.

She'd given him control.

The last thing on his mind at this moment was control, of her, the castle or the pack.

Right now he wanted Katya's cum in his mouth, wanted her writhing against his face as she rode out her orgasm, and wanted to know that he'd been the one to take her there.

"Give it to me," he whispered against her thigh, then flattened his tongue and pressed hard against her clit.

She bucked off the table, grinding her pussy against his tongue and screamed in rapid Romanian.

Fluid poured from her cunt as she rocked against his mouth. He took in her juices, lapping up the tangy flavor while she trembled and bucked beneath him. Her movements drove him crazy and he laid one hand in his lap to rub his aching shaft.

When she relaxed, his cock was more than ready for its part.

He stood and placed his hands on her thighs, leaning over to touch his lips to hers. Whatever reticence she'd started with had long since fled. She wound her fingers in his hair and tugged his face closer for a longer, more intimate kiss. When she licked his lips and chin, tasting her own cum, he shuddered, desperate to sheathe his pulsing shaft in her.

"You ready for this?"

She met his gaze, hers sober and much more restrained than it had been a few moments ago. But she nodded and said, "Yes. I yield. Now fuck me."

His nostrils flared with animal passion, the words he most wanted to hear having been uttered by his mate.

He yanked his shirt off, unbuttoned his jeans and jerked the zipper down, freeing his straining cock from its confines.

Katya's eyes widened and she licked her lips as she stared at his shaft. He stroked it for her slowly, letting the pre-cum ooze from the tip. But rather than swiping it away, he moved closer, rubbing it against the entrance to her sex.

In this position he could see her pussy so clearly, the lips swollen and glistening with her cream. He leaned over her, hovered only inches from her lips and said, "This is mine. Only mine."

With one thrust, he buried himself inside her.

She was so tight, so hot, and he pulsed within her, ready to spill his seed. But he wanted more than just a few seconds of feeling her sweet pussy clamped down around his shaft.

Hell, he wanted an eternity of it.

With a low growl he pulled back and thrust again, this time a little harder, watching as her pussy lips held tight to his shaft when he withdrew, then sucked him back inside to squeeze his pulsing cock.

Resisting the urge to fuck her savagely, he continued to stroke with a gentle rhythm. After all, it was only last night that he'd taken her for the first time.

But she responded to his thrusts by lifting her hips and wrapping her legs around him, forcing his cock deeper.

"Don't treat me like I'll break," she said, anger sparking in her eyes. "Give it to me like you want to...like I want you to."

"You'll be sore."

"I don't care. Fuck me!"

Far be it for him to turn down his woman's request. He reared back and drove hard, then withdrew and powered in again. His balls slapped against her ass as he pushed deeper, faster, taking her with him while he spiraled completely out of control.

Sweat beaded on his brow as he fought the shattering climax that hovered so close. He gritted his teeth, buried his shaft in deeper, listening to the satisfying sounds of the table creaking as it scooted across the floor from the power of his thrusts. His balls banged against her ass, the soft sucking sounds of his cock plunging between her creamy pussy lips driving him to an earth-trembling conclusion. Conner devoured Katya's soft moans that intensified with each stroke of his cock, leaning over to take her mouth in a kiss that spoke of claiming, of possession.

He powered hard and the table moved a few more inches. Katya tore her mouth away from his and screamed, her body shaking as she flooded his balls with her cream. He went with her, howling his pleasure, his animal sounds mixing with hers as she twisted and trembled beneath him.

Conner slid his hands under her buttocks and drove deep, riding out the last tremors of his orgasm with an intensity that made it difficult to remain standing. She'd drained him. Every drop. He was exhausted, exhilarated and, surprisingly, ready to go at it again.

It took a few minutes for him to realize that Katya was squirming lightly. He pushed up on his arms and looked down at her.

"You okay?"

She nodded, but he knew she had to be uncomfortable. Quickly lifting up, he pulled her to a standing position.

Damn, he'd been rough on her. She was still practically a virgin and she'd made him forget that. Then again, she had begged him to be rough.

"Why are you smiling?" she asked, bending down to reach for her discarded clothing.

*Because I'm a stud*. He forced himself not to laugh at himself. "Why do you think I'm smiling?"

She arched a brow, holding her clothes against her body like a shield. "Because you won."

Admittedly, she was partially correct in her assumption. But only partially. He reached for her hand, refusing to yield when she tried to snatch it back. "Come with me."

"You got what you came here for, Conner. We're finished now."

"No, we're not. We're just getting started."

Despite her exasperated sigh, she followed him up the winding staircase to their bedroom.

Katya stood in the doorway, her clothes still draped against her nude body. "Since you insist on occupying this room, I'll be sleeping in another."

She really had no idea what it meant to mate with him. Did she think he'd walk away from her now that they were bonded? Not fucking likely. "I'm not leaving this room and you won't be either. Being mated means we share the same space, the same bed. Even your people will agree with that."

Not giving her time to respond, he brushed past her into the tiled bath, noting that at least the plumbing didn't seem in disrepair. A huge sunken tub cornered the room, a double window above it.

The shower was separate from the tub and big enough for two people. There was a vanity and dressing area, and a huge closet that held no clothes and very few linens.

Conner turned on the water in the tub, adjusting it to a steamy temperature. Then he turned to Katya. "Put your hair up and give me your clothes."

"I can bathe myself," she said, that stubborn chin of hers lifting defiantly.

"Yes, you can. Now indulge me and let me pamper you a bit."

Pamper? No one had ever pampered her before. Why couldn't Conner act like most of the men she knew? They wanted something, they took it. They made no apologies and certainly never lingered with their women afterward. She'd heard enough stories from Elena and the other women here to know how it was supposed to work.

What was wrong with this strange American? He hated her but he acted as if he was happy to be mated to her.

"I need no…pampering, as you call it. Just leave me alone."

He turned to her, reaching for her clothes. She held tight but was no match for his strength as he jerked them away and tossed them in the basket.

He held out his hand and helped her step in the tub. She sank gratefully up to her neck, the scented oils relaxing her tense muscles. Once she settled in, she realized she was lying in the tub naked while he perched on the edge, watching. He still wore his jeans, though he hadn't pulled the zipper up. The dark fur along his lower abdomen caught her attention.

Their coupling had been focused on her body, her pleasure. Other than the ability to view his magnificent chest, she hadn't had the opportunity to see him naked. Recalling last night, she realized that she wanted to see his body.

"What are you thinking about?" he asked, startling her out of her lazy inspection of his body.

"I'm naked."

His eyes glowed when he smiled. "Yes."

"You're not."

"True. Would you like me to remedy that?"

"Yes," she blurted before she had time to think of all the reasons she should say no.

He stood and slipped the jeans off his hips and down his legs, stepping out of them and into the tub with her.

Her eyes widened. "That wasn't what I had in mind!"

Ignoring her, he settled into the water at the opposite end of the tub. "Then what did you have in mind when you asked me to get naked?"

A valid question. One she didn't have an answer to other than the immediate desire to see his body completely uncovered. What had she expected would happen? He'd undress, prance around her bathroom like a fashion model and show off his assets?

She giggled, feeling strangely giddy considering the ramifications of all that had occurred tonight.

Conner leaned back against the tub and maneuvered his legs along the side, fitting his feet next to her thighs.

She tried to draw her knees up, but he caught her ankles, placing them in his lap and massaging the bottoms of her feet. Okay, that didn't feel so bad. She leaned against the rolled pillow attached to the back of the tub, closed her eyes, and let him work his magic.

Thankfully, he seemed content to massage her feet without speaking, allowing her time to regain her bearings and give tonight's events some thought.

How had it all gotten so out of control so quickly? How stupid to think she could ignore him when her body wept for his touch. Her arrogance had cost her tonight. She didn't doubt for a moment that he'd expect her to submit to him now.

He was wrong.

"You're thinking again."

She opened her eyes and met his half smile. "How do you know I'm thinking?"

"You frown when you're in thought. And you bite your bottom lip."

He was right. "You're very observant."

"It's my business to be observant."

"You examine too much. You interfere."

He shook his head and continued to rub the bottom of her feet. "Tell me about the Carpathian wolf population."

"What do you want to know?"

"Everything. Who's involved, who's endangering them. Tell me about your government, about the hunters."

She heaved a sigh. "Wolves have been fighting for survival for centuries here. Though the killing isn't as rampant as it once was, there seems to be a resurgence over the past decade."

"Why?"

"Fear, mostly. The numbers of wolves are exaggerated by government groups who bow to pressure from the hunting lobbies, making it easier to authorize free hunting to reduce the population."

"To protect farmers' livestock from wolf attacks."

She snorted. "It's more likely that the hunters are using that as an excuse to do what they do best, what they love to do."

"Aren't wolves protected as an endangered species here?"

"They're supposed to be, but keep in mind that in wolf form we are inherent roamers. We cross borders. Protected in one country can mean hunted in another."

"We have a lot of work to do."

She wanted to object, tell him that she had everything under control, but arguing with him while they both sat naked in the tub wouldn't be a good idea. As it was, she felt more vulnerable than she liked. He already knew more about her than anyone ever had.

She couldn't quite figure him out. He was alpha, that was certain, yet there was an underlying tenderness that confused her.

Most men she could predict. Not Conner Devlin.

That made him dangerous.

Especially the way he touched her, sliding his hands ever so slowly from her feet to her ankles and higher. The sensuous way he massaged her calves made her libido once again rise up and demand to be satisfied.

She tried to concentrate on making polite conversation, which was difficult considering the way his gaze roamed over her body. Her nipples puckered and peeked up out of the water.

He glanced from her breasts to her face and grinned.

"I want more," he stated.

She did, too. A revelation she found quite disconcerting.

"But not tonight. You'll be too sore."

She fought back the disappointment at his statement. He was being logical. Of course she was sore. That didn't make her desire lessen.

Nor his, considering his clearly visible erection.

He was right anyway. She shouldn't want him, shouldn't think with lust instead of her brain. Taking a step back to gather her wits was the smart thing to do. The last thing she needed was to end up lost in this man's magnetic charm.

Just because she'd been fucked didn't mean she had to change her entire life. Conner might think he was in charge now, but she hadn't given up control just yet.

# Chapter Eight

ဆာ

After he'd pulled Katya from the bath, Conner grabbed one of the large towels and dried her off, trying to ignore the urge to take her again.

Because he knew "again" would lead to more "agains" until she'd be so sore she'd regret letting him touch her.

But with her skin flushed pink and warm from the bath, the high color in her sculpted cheekbones and the way her gaze raked over his naked body, he began to weaken.

This was his mate, after all, the woman who answered his primal urges. He couldn't help but want her.

When he lifted her in his arms and carried her from the room, she pushed against his chest.

"Conner. I am not injured. I'm perfectly capable of walking."

Had no one ever romanced the beautiful princess before? Cherished her? Obviously no man had fucked her before him, but there was a lot more to a relationship than just sex.

"I know you can walk. I like the feel of you in my arms."

She blinked, seemingly at a loss for words.

Good. He made a mental note to keep her unbalanced. She already spent way too much time thinking. Logically, too, he'd bet, instead of listening to her body, her heart.

Not that her heart was involved in this, any more than his. Like the arranged marriages of the old days, what they did was because they were required to, not because they'd dated, got to know each other and then made the choice to be together.

No, the lupine way was much different. It was entirely possible for two people to loathe each other and still be unable to resist the urge to mate.

He placed her on top of the covers. She sat up and curled her legs to one side, staring up at him.

"I thought we might…explore each other a bit."

One perfectly arched brow lifted. "Explore?"

"Yes." He climbed onto the bed and she scooted back a bit. In answer, he moved closer and picked up her hand, bringing it to his lips to kiss her palm.

Her breath hitched when his tongue touched the inside of her hand, her fingers curling around his jaw. He licked her palm, and her pulse quickened.

"There's a lot more to sex than penetration," he explained.

"Yes. I know. You licked my pussy and I came."

His cock jerked to life at the memory of her sweet taste against his tongue. "Yes, there's that, but I was in a bit of a hurry earlier. Now, we have time."

"You mean we'll be doing it again?"

"Not fucking, no. I was pretty rough with you tonight and I don't want to make you sore."

"I liked it rough."

Christ. Katya was full of surprises. "You did, huh?"

"Yes." Her voice lowered to an almost whisper, as if she regretted revealing her intimate thoughts.

"I'm glad. I enjoyed fucking you. Your pussy is tight and hot, Katya. You were made for my cock."

The pink in her cheeks deepened. "You are very strange."

He laughed. "Is that good or bad?"

Her lips curled in a grin. "That remains to be seen."

Feeling relaxed for the first time since he'd started this journey, he moved closer, reaching out and caressing her cheek, mesmerized with the satiny feel of her skin, the way her breasts rose and fell and the utter innocence reflected in her brandy-colored eyes. When her lids drifted shut, her long, dark eyelashes brushed the tops of her cheekbones.

The woman was absolutely perfect and completely beguiling.

He was in deep shit here. He wanted her with a fierce desire that was foreign to him, as was the protectiveness that came over him whenever he looked at her.

She was his. Not like a possession, but like a mate. A soul mate. His woman. God, the thoughts in his head would drive him insane if he took time to analyze them.

He'd always gone with his gut feelings. And his gut feeling told him to take her again, plant his seed within her, build a dynasty with her.

Fuck. He hadn't counted on this.

"You're thinking again."

He looked up, not realizing he'd drifted off into some weird zone of deep thought. Recalling that he'd said the exact same thing to her earlier, he nodded. "That I am."

"About…?"

Somehow he doubted she really wanted to know what he was thinking. "I was thinking about you." And that was as much as he'd tell.

"What about me?"

"I'm just wondering about your experience with men."

"Oh. That. I have none, as you well know."

Was she worried that she'd disappointed him? Hell, she'd nearly killed him. If she was this hot while still innocent, she'd be the death of him once she gained more experience.

He leaned in and brushed his lips against hers, tasting the brandy that still lingered on her lips. "Baby, you were amazing. You did notice that I came buckets inside you, didn't you?"

There was that blush on her cheeks again. "Yes, I did notice that you seemed to enjoy it. But I thought men came regardless of the woman's experience. Isn't one orifice just as good as another? A tight squeeze and you'll get off?"

"Whoa. You don't pull any punches, do you?"

She frowned. "I don't understand. Punches?"

"It's a phrase that means you say exactly what's on your mind."

"Oh. Then yes, I do."

"Well, you're wrong. There's coming and then there's *coming*. When it's really good, a man can come so hard he can feel it down to his toes."

She glanced down at his feet and he had to force himself to hold back a laugh, knowing she wouldn't understand. "Yeah, you did that to me."

And if she kept looking at him like she wanted to eat him alive, he'd have an orgasm just like the first one very soon.

As a matter of fact, that wasn't a bad idea at all.

"Touch me, Katya."

She curled her fingers into her palms, her gaze roaming from his face to his feet. When she looked up again, curiosity filled her eyes.

"Anywhere you want to," he answered in response to her unspoken question.

She started at his hair, tangling her fingers within it.

"I've wanted to do that since that first night outside the hotel. Your hair shines in the night like it has a silver halo surrounding it." When she tugged on the back, he groaned, wanting her to do that when he fucked her.

But he held still, allowing her to explore, to learn about a man's body.

His body.

Starting at his face, she traced the line of his jaw and ran her fingers over his lips before moving down to his neck. When she reached his chest she moved closer, tangling her fingers into the crisp hairs there. He sucked in a breath when her fingernails lightly scraped his nipples, making them stand out.

"Your nipples get erect, just like…"

"Like yours? Yeah. I like it when you touch them. Makes my cock twitch."

Her gaze followed his statement and she circled his nipples, keeping watch of his cock. He teased her by making it jerk upward, laughing when her eyes widened.

"Your cock feels the touch of my fingers on your nipples?"

"Yeah." Hell, his cock felt every one of her caresses, hardening, throbbing, lengthening. But still, he didn't move to touch her, although he was dying to toss her onto her back and bury his shaft in her hot cunt.

When she bent her head toward his chest, her little pink tongue darting out to trace the flat nipples, he dug his fingers into the coverlet, forcing himself to hold still.

She swiped one nipple, covering her lips over it and suckling it gently.

"Oh fuck, that's good," he said, fighting to breathe through the erotic sensations.

She looked up at him, her eyes dark with arousal, then bent to the other nipple and did the same.

He'd have to turn the tables on her sometime very soon and torture her the same way.

"Lie down on the bed," she commanded.

He lay on his back and locked his hands behind his head, hoping like hell he could resist the urge to take her. His cock jutted straight up, a drop of pre-cum appearing at the tip.

He sent her mental signals to lick him, but he wasn't going to force her to take his cock into her mouth.

Not yet, anyway. Later, when she was experienced and he had control and dominance, then he'd tell her to suck him. Until then, he'd just have to settle for—

"Holy shit, Katya!" He nearly bolted off the bed when she answered his silent pleas and licked the drop of fluid off the tip of his cock.

Damn, she was surprising.

She smiled, licking her lips. "Salty. I like the flavor."

He was wrong. Experience be damned, she was already killing him.

She bent over him again, her hair brushing his thighs. She kept her gaze focused on his face as she covered her lips over the tip of his shaft, then slowly slid down, engulfing him with her hot mouth.

With a low groan he lifted his hips, driving his cock into the deepest recesses of her throat. She took him greedily, wrapping her fingers around the base and stroking him as she sucked.

When she pulled away, she said, "Interesting texture. Hard, but soft as velvet at the same time. Especially here." She circled the tip with her finger, then wrapped both hands around him and stroked upward, bending down to lave the slit of his cock with her tongue.

"Lord, woman. Are you sure you haven't done this before?" He tangled his fingers in her hair and thrust forward, matching the rhythm of her strokes.

She sucked him deep, her hands moving over his shaft in a twisting motion, pulling him deeper and deeper into her hot mouth until his balls tightened and throbbed.

"Let go, Katya, I'm going to come," he managed, his chest heaving with the force of his labored breaths.

But she held on, squeezing him tighter, releasing one hand to search for his balls.

When she cupped and massaged them, he exploded into her mouth, pumping his cream down her throat. Just like the first time, his orgasm rocked him from head to toe, making him shudder and lose control.

She swallowed and continued to suck until his cock began to soften, then sat on her heels and licked her lips, a satisfied grin on her face.

"I had no idea that sucking a man could be so arousing."

She *was* going to be the death of him.

Katya felt like she'd died and gone to heaven. Having access to Conner's body, his willingness to let her do whatever she wanted, was like waking up on Christmas morning with the gift of her dreams under the tree.

She'd always wanted to touch a hard cock, taste it, feel the shaft in her mouth while she pleasured a man. She'd read books. Hot, erotic stories of lust and passion, her mind awash in visuals of what a man and woman could do together.

But her youthful fantasies had been squelched by the death of her parents. Once she'd taken over the pack, she knew she couldn't experiment, couldn't play, couldn't learn about sex.

When one was an alpha, sex also carried the burden of responsibility. So she kept her distance.

Besides, none of the men she knew intrigued her enough to even think about mating. She'd always felt like she was waiting for "the one". The one alpha who would take her, dominate her and fuck her, whether she liked it or not.

Her fantasy had become a reality in a way she'd never expected.

And now the dominant male of her dreams had exposed his underbelly to her, lying immobile while she explored his body with her hands and her mouth.

She shuddered, so aroused she could hardly sit still. There was so much she had to learn, so much she wanted to explore. .

"Come here," Conner said, his voice low.

She braced her hands on either side of his face, leaned down and kissed him.

He devoured her lips with his mouth, sliding his tongue inside, mimicking the same long strokes he'd used when his cock was inside her earlier.

She reached for his shaft but he grabbed her wrist and pulled her hand away. When she leaned back to look at him, he said, "Straddle my face and let me lick you."

Her body heated, juices seeping from the swollen lips of her pussy. Her clit ached for his mouth, desperate for Conner to take her over the edge again. But like this? Her face burned with the knowledge that she could be so intimate with him.

"Come on," he urged, squeezing the flesh of her hip. "Climb on my face and ride my tongue, baby."

Unable to resist the lure of release, she straddled his face, aligning her pussy over his mouth. His tongue snaked out and licked her slit. She cried out and leaned forward, reaching for the headboard, needing something to hold onto.

Carefully braced, she began to rock slowly against Conner's tongue, finding the movements that placed her clit within reach of his magic. He grabbed onto her buttocks and slid her pussy back and forth over his tongue. Exquisite sensations sparked deep in her womb at the visual before her. Conner's mouth buried over her clit, his tongue swirling along her sensitive nerve endings.

What a picture this must make. She couldn't believe she acted so wantonly, so out of control. Was this really her, or did Conner draw this wild response from her?

As she drew closer and closer to completion, her primal urges took over. She shuddered, the changes coming upon her without warning. Shocked, she looked down at Conner. His eyes were closed but he growled against her sex as if he knew exactly what she felt.

Her blood burned, her skin on fire with the need to shift. She fought it back. Now was not the time to run wild.

But it was so damn hard, especially when his fingers dug into her buttocks and he quickened his pace, sliding her back and forth over his mouth, capturing her clit and sucking it between his lips.

She cried out when her orgasm washed over her, digging her nails into the headboard, the lupine part of her drawing her claws to rake against the wooden bed frame. Conner held tight to her hips and slid his tongue inside her cunt, lapping up the cream that spilled from her.

Exhausted, she crawled off him and collapsed onto the bed, letting him draw her against his chest.

She settled in, looked down and noticed his cock was rock-hard again. When she looked at him, he smiled, his face wet with her juices.

"You turn me on, Katya. I can't help that I want you."

She moved to touch him but he gently pushed her arm away, grabbing her hand and tucking it inside his.

"Sleep," he said, kissing the top of her head. "We have forever to get to know each other."

Forever. Both a comforting and frightening word. She lay there silently, listening to the night sounds outside the castle and focusing on the rhythmic rise and fall of Conner's chest.

He was right. It had already been an eventful day and night. Yet there was so much she wanted to experience and a part of her wondered if she and Conner were, in fact, bound for "forever".

*Stop thinking, Katya. Stop worrying about the future. Things will unfold as they should.*

She knew her inner voice was right and she should stop worrying about it.

Change wasn't always a bad thing. Maybe she and Conner could work things out after all. They'd certainly made a good start. They were compatible sexually, that much was certain. Whether they could come to terms in other areas remained to be seen.

She closed her eyes and let the sound of his heartbeat against her ear lull her to sleep.

* * * * *

Katya woke to sunlight streaming in the windows.

She sat up and looked around. Okay, she was alone in the bed. Where was Conner?

The clock on the wall stated it was ten in the morning. She'd slept way too long.

Tossing off the covers, she took a shower and dressed in jeans and a sweater, feeling more relaxed than she had in a very long time.

Last night she'd slept the entire night instead of waking several times to stare out the window and wonder what crises would arrive on her doorstep by morning.

Conner had exhausted her completely and she'd slept soundly, without the nightmares that typically disturbed her.

Perhaps having sex was going to be therapeutic as well as enjoyable.

She entered the kitchen but he wasn't there. Coffee was, though, and she poured herself a cup, taking it with her as she wandered the rooms in search of her mate.

Voices came from her office down the hall, and she followed the sounds, opening the door to a full room.

No one ever entered her private office without her being there. Until now. Conner was seated at her desk, Noah standing next to him on one side, Elena on the other.

Elena leaned toward Conner as he whispered in her ear. When he finished speaking, Elena stood and began giving orders to the men assembled in the room, who nodded and left.

Conner looked up as one of the men said her name as he passed by.

"Morning," he said, seemingly right at home with her papers on her desk, giving orders to her people. "Elena is translating for me. We've gotten a good start."

Her mellow mood vanished in an instant. Anger filled her to the point of threatening to topple the cup of coffee in her trembling hand. She forced herself to maintain control. "What exactly do you think you're doing in here?"

"I'm working."

She didn't like the smug look he gave her. Was this the same man who'd bathed her and pleasured her last night? Placing her cup on a nearby table, she entered the room and stopped in front of her desk. "Working on what?"

"I've made arrangements for a crew to bring supplies and manpower to start erecting sturdier fencing around the castle property." He grinned and laced his fingers behind his head, leaning back in her chair. "Trust me, it'll be wolf-proof."

She had no idea what he was talking about. "We haven't discussed that."

"No, we haven't. We have to protect the population here from both the inside and the outside. Keep the wolves contained and keep the hunters out."

"I see." So nice of him to completely take over. She should have thought of mating sooner. It could have done wonders for her beauty sleep.

"He has some very good ideas, Katya," Elena said. "I am very impressed with how quickly he has made arrangements for our protection. You should see all that he's accomplished this morning."

She glared her cousin into silence. Yes, she could well imagine what he'd done. The evidence of it sat at *her* desk, in *her* chair, in *her* office. Conner had already taken over the pack, the castle, the land…everything that she claimed as hers.

"Leave," she commanded Elena. "And take everyone with you."

Elena had the gall to look down at Conner, who nodded.

She turned to Noah and said, "You can get out, too. I need to speak to Conner alone."

Noah smirked and crossed his arms, clearly not about to go anywhere on her orders. Elena shuffled the rest of them out of the room quickly, her eyes downcast as she hurried past Katya.

Conner looked up at Noah. "Go ahead and get started on the things we talked about. We'll meet in about an hour and go over the details."

Noah nodded and left the room, inclining his head in a bow as he walked past her and closed the door behind him.

The latch had no sooner clicked in place than she turned to Conner and said, "Get out of my chair."

Conner smiled. "Why?"

"Get out of my chair," she said again, barely able to contain the fury rolling through her blood. Her claws shot from her nails, her vision clouded by the change coming over her. She fought it back, but not before a low growl poured from her chest.

He stood and grasped her arms. "This is what you wanted, wasn't it? When you allowed me to fuck a virgin princess and be forced to become your mate, this was what you had in mind, right?"

She jerked away from his hold and stepped to her desk, sitting down and looking at him. "This," she said, sweeping her hand over her desk, "is mine."

"Not anymore. I'm the alpha male. I'm also the one with all the money. You wanted the Devlins, baby, you got 'em. The whole package. Including one very in charge alpha here."

"It's symbolic, you moron," she retorted. "Are you so dense that you can't pick up on that? I'm Braslieu royalty. You have no say here."

"Tell that to your people. They take orders from me just fine. I think they've been craving a man in charge around here since your father died. They seemed...how should I say it? Relieved."

She longed to scratch that smirk right off his face. "You may have fucked me last night and claimed alpha status, but that doesn't mean you take over my duties."

"Actually, that's exactly what I'll be doing. I'll make all the decisions now."

"No, you will not. We will discuss things together and make joint decisions based on my input. I know this area, this government and my people, better than you. You will defer to me in all decisions."

Conner laughed and crossed his arms. "It's not going to work that way. You can tell me everything I need to know, but I'll take it from there."

How could she have been so blind? He'd played her last night. Now that he was stuck here, he was playing prime alpha to the hilt. Whatever happened between them last night wasn't emotional, wasn't bonding. She'd been nothing more than a fuck. She meant nothing more than a means to an end, the result being power over the wolves of Braslieu.

He'd done a fine job of lulling her into thinking they'd work together as a team. How stupid was she? One good fuck and she'd given everything to him. No, she *hadn't* given. He'd taken.

"Get up from the desk, Katya. You've had your tantrum, now let me get some work done."

"Don't you *dare* patronize me!" She slammed her hands on the desk and stood, leaning over to make sure he understood exactly who was in charge. She bared her teeth, allowing the wolf within her to surface. "I rule Braslieu, not you. I will make the decisions, not you. And I will tell my people what to do. *Not* you!"

She'd shouted the last sentence to get her point across, her voice low and husky with the change.

But Conner didn't flinch. Instead, he placed his palms on his end of the desk and leaned over so their noses nearly touched.

His eyes darkened with lupine change, teeth elongating, his jaw jutting out. Claws dug into the end of the desk as he growled a warning. "Don't undermine what I do, Katya. It's for the protection of all the wolves here. I am alpha now, make no mistake. I do not need, nor will I ever ask your permission to do what I think is necessary."

"We'll see about that." She turned her head to the door and shouted for her personal guards. In a matter of moments, they came through the door.

"I want you to remove Conner from the room," she said, turning to Conner and offering a smug smile. Soon enough, he'd see who was in charge here.

But they stood there, confused frowns on their faces.

"Did you hear me? Remove him, now!"

"Princess, he is the alpha. We cannot," Nicolai said, an apologetic look on his face.

"*I* am alpha here and I command you to remove him."

Jens shook his head, not making eye contact with her. "We cannot. The lupine laws are clear. You have mated with Conner Devlin. He is alpha male and we take our orders from him now."

This was unbelievable. They looked to Conner, who nodded his head and inclined it toward the doorway. The guards made a quick exit.

Seething fury kept the wolf present. She didn't even bother to try and hide the ferocity of her anger. She had half a mind to pounce on him and *really* let him see how angry she was.

She'd lose the battle, of course. No way could she match his physical strength. But she'd get a few bites and scratches in first.

"I don't know what you said to them, but I assume you were asking them to move me out of here. That won't do you any good, Katya. They know who the alpha is now."

This wasn't happening. Yesterday she was in charge. Today she was…nothing. And why? Because she'd fucked an alpha wolf?

"I'm not here to harm anyone, baby."

"Don't call me baby. In fact, don't even speak to me."

He skirted the desk and came around to her side. She moved away.

"Katya," he said, his voice soft as if he was speaking to a child. "We may be adversarial in the way I got here, but now that I'm in place I want to help. We don't have to do battle."

"I'm not doing battle with you, Conner. I'm not doing anything with you. You've come in here and taken away everything that is mine. That's unacceptable."

"I've taken nothing away. Believe me, joining with the Devlins was the wisest decision you could make for your people. They understand that now."

"I didn't *join* with you! It was a mistake!"

He stared at her with a blank expression of innocence that infuriated her. She was getting nowhere with this hardheaded American. "Just stay the hell out of my way, Conner. And don't touch or change a goddamned thing around here! This is my castle, my people, and you do not have my permission to do anything!"

Before she did something incredibly weak, like burst into tears, she stormed from the room, flinging the door open to find Noah, Elena and a dozen of her people waiting outside. No doubt, they'd heard everything.

Elena looked at her with sympathy, as did the rest of them.

They pitied her! She must look like a fool. Half-human, half-lupine, and wrestling with female emotions that threatened to send her into a curled up ball of misery.

This was all too much.

"You follow him?" she asked, inclining her head to the closed door.

No one looked her in the eye.

"Cousin, you know the lupine laws," Elena said, her voice quiet.

"You are all fools," she spat, not even trying to hide the disgust in her voice.

She turned and walked down the hall with her head held high, refusing to swipe at the tears that pooled in her eyes and slid slowly down her cheeks.

The wolf within her retreated as melancholy replaced anger.

In the blink of an eye, she'd lost it all.

God help her people now, because the Devlins didn't have a clue.

# Chapter Nine

ജ

Conner stood at the window of the office, looking out over the thick green and gold forests below and wondering what the fuck had just happened between him and Katya.

Last night it seemed as if they might have struck a tenuous peace, both in bed and out. They'd shared a night of great sex, followed by an easy conversation that led him to believe things might work out for them.

He'd pleasured her that much he knew for certain. She'd come several times, each time more intense than the last. Then she'd slept soundly in his arms last night, tucked against his side as if she'd spent her entire life there.

He'd assumed everything had been settled between them, but then she exploded because he sat at her desk? He just didn't get it.

The door opened and Noah slipped in, closing it behind him and crossing his arms.

"Well, you handled that well, brother. Anything else you care to fuck up or was that your big one of the day?"

"What the hell are you talking about? You know I'm doing exactly what I'm supposed to. Setting things in motion to protect the wolves here. I'm doing my job, Noah."

"I know what your job is. I'm talking about Katya."

"What about her?"

"You screwed up."

Conner leaned his hip against the window ledge. "How?"

"She was in charge here. You took over without even consulting or warning her what would happen. Then you made decisions and didn't ask for her advice."

"I don't need her advice. I also didn't ask to end up here, but it looks like that's what's going to happen, so I might as well take charge and get things rolling. I know what needs to be done."

Noah shook his head and approached, sitting next to him on the ledge. "You don't know shit about women, Conner. You never have. All you do is fuck them. You never consider their feelings."

Conner's jaw dropped. Who was this stranger across from him? Noah waxing philosophical about women's feelings? "And where did you amass this great knowledge about women?"

Noah smirked. "I pay attention to details. It's my job to read people so that I can manipulate a situation. One of the things I've learned along the way is how to use a woman's emotions to my advantage. And you learn that by observing, by knowing what makes them happy and what pisses them off."

"Uh-huh. Well, Katya knew what she was doing when she set out to play her little game. She gambled and long term, I win. I'm the alpha here now, and the sooner she gets used to it the better."

"This is all because you feel trapped into something you didn't get to decide for yourself. This is your revenge, right?

"No, this is business."

"Bullshit. It's payback. So you'd rather have the princess at odds with you instead of on your side."

"There are no sides. We're all the same pack now. She's my mate. It's her duty to follow my rules."

"That's all well and good for lupine laws, Con, but we're also partially human. And that means emotion comes into play. Women's emotions. You don't want to fuck with those, trust me."

"I know what I'm doing," Conner said, moving back to the desk.

"You don't have a goddamned idea what you're doing. This venture will be a helluva lot more successful with Katya's cooperation. Without it, you've got one major battle on your hands."

Heaving an exasperated sigh, Conner looked up at Noah. "So what do you suggest I do?"

Noah's lips curled in a smirk. "First thing you've got to do is pull your foot out of your mouth. You're going to have to learn that being alpha doesn't necessarily mean that you bully everyone into doing it your way. Besides, Katya knows this area. She can help you."

"I can figure it out on my own. Plus, her people will help me."

"They will, but only because they're honor bound to do so. If they see you mistreating their princess, you could end up with a mutiny someday. Hell, Con, you had her right where you wanted her. Then you had to go act like an ass. You think they didn't notice how you treated her like she was nothing? Don't you think they're going to wonder if you're really here for their best interests, or your own?"

Noah had a point. Maybe he'd been a little bit too domineering with her. But dammit, it galled him that he'd been so easily manipulated. Maybe he had been lashing out at her instead of acting logically. "I suppose it wouldn't hurt to enlist her aid."

"Yeah, if she ever speaks to you again. Hope you got a good fuck last night, bro. It'll probably be the last one you get for a while."

Noah turned and left the room, his snicker echoing down the hall.

Shit. He didn't need this. Why couldn't things run more smoothly?

And how the hell was he supposed to figure out how to deal with a woman and her emotions? He'd never been able to fathom that mystery before.

He knew how to treat them in the bedroom. Never had any complaints there.

But business was different, and this was business. Didn't Katya see that?

He glared at the phone, not wanting to make the call but knowing he had no choice. Before he chickened out he lifted the receiver and dialed the international codes to the U.S., hoping she'd actually answer her cell phone for once.

"This had better be good. It's the goddamned middle of the night."

"Hello, Chantal." He ignored her surly attitude. His sister was always grouchy when she woke up.

"Conner, somebody had better be dead for you to be making this call."

Yeah. Him, if he didn't get Katya figured out. "No one's dead. Sorry to disappoint you."

"Then what is it?"

Her biting tone made him smile. God he loved his sister. He flinched as he blurted out the words. "I need woman advice."

He rolled his eyes at the sound of Chantal's hysterical laughter. Okay, he only loved her sometimes. Other times she was a real ball-busting pain in the ass.

* * * * *

By nightfall, Conner had at least made some inroads on the construction aspect of the mission.

That had been the easy part. After Chantal had chewed him a new asshole and pointed out all the ways he'd screwed up with Katya, he figured the hard part was about to begin.

Admittedly, both Noah and Chantal had been right. In his zeal to prove to Katya that he really was the big dick in charge, he'd handled the situation less than responsibly. Chantal had reminded him that the alpha female of the pack was his biggest ally. She could also be his worst enemy. The last thing he needed was a mate who couldn't stand the sight of him.

Now he had to work to rebuild the trust he'd broken. As strong-willed as Katya was, that wasn't going to be an easy task. He'd tried to see her today, but she'd been busy, unavailable, or simply unwilling to take a minute to exchange two words with him.

Her glare had been lethal, the "drop dead" signals quite clear. Her anger was palpable, and now that he'd had the chance to replay this morning's events, he couldn't blame her.

Sometimes he was a prick. Especially as it related to business and what he wanted to get done. In his work, nothing and no one got in his way. Only Katya wasn't in his way. She was an important part of the pack and he was going to have to do one hell of a job of backpedaling to undo the damage he'd done this morning.

First thing he'd done was enlist Noah and Elena's aid in once again emptying the castle of all inhabitants for the night. Noah was more than happy to shift and shack up with Elena in the woods for the night. The rest of the castle population disappeared, and he had no idea where. But Elena assured him they'd be alone for the evening.

He finished up in the kitchen, then popped the cork on a bottle of wine he'd found in the cellars. Fires had been lit in all the fireplaces, rendering the castle warm and toasty.

The table was set, the wine breathing. Now he had to find Katya and convince her to join him. Elena had told him that Katya was holed up in her room, unwilling to come downstairs.

Taking a deep breath, Conner stepped through the door to the bedroom.

Katya was sitting up in bed reading. She didn't even bother to look up at him.

"I made dinner."

She ignored him.

"I'd like you to join me."

Still ignoring him.

"I opened a bottle of wine."

Clearly she'd gone deaf.

Or she was ignoring him.

Deciding to try a different tactic, he said, "Princess Katya, would you do me the honor of dining with me this evening? There are important matters related to the land and the wolves that I'd like to discuss with you."

Finally she looked up, her eyes as cold as a mountain winter. "Why are you dressed up?"

"I thought it would be nice if we had a special dinner tonight. Everyone in the castle is gone and we're alone. We can...talk."

She frowned. "Why do you want to talk to me about anything? I thought you had it all under control."

*Touché.* And he'd deserved that one, too. "It's important. Please."

Damn, it was hard to beg. But Chantal told him he'd have to kiss ass, and most likely all night long, whether he liked it or not. Then, if he was really, really lucky, she might start talking to him again.

"You have to eat anyway. Might as well have dinner with me."

"I can eat up here."

"Katya, I need your advice."

The book dropped to the bed and her shoulders hunched in a big sigh.

"Very well."

She slipped off the bed and started to follow him from the room, but he stopped her.

"Would you mind wearing a dress?"

Arching a brow, she said, "Don't press your luck, Conner. I said I'd eat with you, not parade around in a dress for your benefit."

"You have beautiful legs. I'd love to see them."

"Is that an order from the alpha?" she said, sarcasm dripping from her voice.

"Will it work if I say yes?"

Judging from the "fuck off" look he'd just received, it didn't work at all.

"Get out, Conner."

Shit. Chantal said not to push her. It would only piss her off more.

"I understand. I guess I'll just have to figure this out on my own. Goodnight."

He turned and left the room, heading back into the kitchen and pouring himself a large glass of wine. He downed it in one gulp, then poured another, determined to enjoy the dinner he'd prepared.

It wasn't like he cooked a meal every goddamned day.

As soon as he'd finished loading his plate with steak, potatoes and vegetables, Katya walked in.

No dress, but at least she was here. That was progress.

"Well, are we going to talk?"

He nodded. "If you'd like to go sit in the dining room, I'll bring our plates and drinks in."

She nodded and whirled around, teasing him with a glimpse of her ass in tight black pants.

Lord, she had a sexy walk.

After he'd carried their dinner and drinks into the dining room, he pulled a chair next to her. He'd lit candles earlier, and their glow reflected off the soft dark waves of her hair, illuminating her face. Why couldn't he concentrate on her beauty, on the way her pulse beat against her neck, instead of how to extract himself from this mess his big mouth had gotten him in?

He lifted his glass and said, "To a successful union between the Braslieu and Devlin packs."

She didn't toast, instead looked down at her plate and began to eat.

At least she didn't complain about the food. She ate well, too, and didn't pick like some women did. He hated when a woman left her food on the plate, like it was some great sin to eat a meal. Wolves ate for strength, knowing they'd need it to survive. A picky woman wouldn't last an hour in the woods with a pack of wolves.

They ate in silence. Conner struggled for an opening, wondering how he was going to broach the subject of his behavior earlier.

When they'd finished the meal, she drained her glass and he refilled it. She swirled the red liquid around the glass and stared at him expectantly.

Christ, he'd never been nervous before. How goddamned hard was it to utter an apology?

"I behaved like a prick this morning, Katya. I'm sorry. This is all very new to me and I handled it badly."

She arched a brow, but said nothing.

"I'm used to people staying out of my way and following my lead in business. I went ahead and made decisions that I thought were best for the pack. I have to do that as alpha and you know it."

Still no reaction.

"I'm still more than a bit pissed off about not having a choice in who I mated. But that's done now, and I could use your help. You're the native here, and I'm the outsider. I should have asked you to consult instead of charging ahead and making decisions."

It galled him to apologize for being himself, but he swallowed the bitter taste and forged on. "I didn't consider your feelings in this. I won't make the same mistake again."

He waited while she looked at him for a minute. Then she said, "I accept your apology."

"Thank you." One hill climbed, about a thousand more to go.

He stood and reached out for her. She looked down at his hand and then back up to his face.

"I accepted your apology, Conner. Let's leave it at that."

She stood without taking his hand and took her plate to the kitchen. He followed her, watching the soft sway of her hips, his cock coming to life.

Now was not a good time for an erection. He had a feeling more apologizing was in order.

"Come with me," he said, not reaching out to touch her this time. Grabbing the wine and their glasses, he moved them to the living room and turned on the old stereo. Soft music played, a tune unfamiliar to him but obviously not to Katya as she turned and stared at the speakers.

"This is a love song." She looked at him accusingly, as if he purposely chose this particular song in order to torture her.

"Is it? I found some CDs. I don't read your language, so I just put one on."

"It's my favorite music. My parents loved it. They'd dance in here, sometimes late into the night. I would watch from the stairs as my father held my mother close and moved her slowly around the room."

She seemed lost in her memories as she continued to stare at the stereo. He came up behind her, stopping just short of reaching for her.

"Dance with me, Katya."

She shook her head. "No."

Now he did touch, sliding his hands up and down her arms. She shivered, but didn't turn around.

"I want you," he whispered against her ear, breathing in her scent that no perfume could mimic. She smelled of wildflowers, sunlight and heavenly woman.

"You'll have to get off with another female."

His hands stilled and he turned her to face him. "What?"

"You heard me. You're never going to touch me again."

Obviously he'd been wrong about the headway he thought he'd made with her. "Katya, I said I was sorry."

"I know. And I'm sure you meant it. But I was foolish enough to let my guard down once. I won't make the same mistake twice."

"We're mated."

"Indeed we are. And when it is necessary to procreate, I will allow it. But for fun and fucking? No. You'll have to go to someone else for that."

All this had been for nothing. She really hadn't forgiven him.

"I won't be going to anyone else for sex, Katya. I only want you."

"You can't have me."

He advanced on her, taking her into his arms and pulling her against him. The time for listening to advice was over. He might consult her on matters related to the castle and wolves, but in this he wouldn't be defied. "I chose you as my mate, Katya. Make no mistake. We will make love, and often. You can argue with me about anything else, but not this."

She stiffened and pushed against his chest, but he held her firmly. "So you plan to rape me?"

His lips curled into a smile. "No, honey. I'm not Peter. I won't be taking what you don't willingly give me."

"Then we're at an impasse, because I don't intend to give you anything."

"Katya, I know your body. I can smell when you're aroused, I know your needs."

She was tense in his arms, but her body told him what she refused to admit.

She wanted him. Her scent gave her away. Sweet, tangy, desire filled the air around them, that musky perfume of aroused female. She might be ticked off at him right now, but she was also hot, aroused and primed for sex.

He'd just have to show her that she couldn't deny herself the pleasure she so desperately craved.

"You want me," he said, leaning in to inhale her scent. When he licked the pulse point at her neck, she shuddered.

"I don't."

"You lie." He kissed his way from her neck to her shoulder, slipping the sweater down her arms, then drawing the strap of her flimsy lace chemise down.

"No, Conner. I don't want this," she whispered, but her heart wasn't in the protest.

The key was to take it slow, to build up to the passion he knew was locked away inside her.

If he took her now, she'd respond eventually, but she'd hate him for showing her as weak. It was time to start paying attention to her signals instead of rushing head first like a bull in heat.

No matter how painful it would to be to hold back.

He pulled the strap up over her shoulder and stepped away. "Come sit down with me and have a drink."

Her eyes widened, then narrowed, as if she'd been surprised he'd stopped. He sat next to her, sipping his wine, memorizing the lines of her body and the way her hair fell over her breasts.

But he didn't touch her.

And she didn't speak, nor did she move toward him.

She did drink her wine, leaned her head against the sofa and closed her eyes.

He wondered where her mind wandered as the soft sounds of violins played on the stereo. Was she transported back to her childhood, watching her parents dance in this room, or was she wishing a more grown-up fantasy to come true?

What did Katya want? What would it take to make her happy? To trust him? To live in contentment with him?

Too bad he didn't know the answer to any of those questions. It certainly would make this easier.

Then he realized that Katya didn't really know him at all. And how could she trust someone she knew nothing about?

Which gave him idea. He never talked about his family with anyone. But if he and Katya were mated, she'd need to know everything about him.

And maybe, just maybe, he could make some inroads with her this way.

"Both my parents' families came from Europe," he said, figuring the best place to start was from the beginning. "The Devlin wolves are from Ireland. My great-great-grandfather immigrated to the United States in the hopes that the land of opportunity would afford his pack the chance to expand and grow. My mother's family came from England in the early eighteen hundreds. Their pack was already established by the time my father's family arrived in America. When my parents met, the merger between the Wainrights and the Devlins was thought to be good business. Good for the lupine society as a whole."

Katya didn't speak, but she hadn't gotten up and left the room, either. He took a long swallow of wine and continued.

"My parents have continued the tradition of their families. I have three brothers and a sister. Jason, the oldest, is a senator in Washington, D.C. His primary goal is to ensure legislation to protect the wolves. He just recently became engaged to his mate, a full human who has agreed to become lupine."

"They allow that?" she asked.

"Yes. Unusual, of course, but my parents aren't going to stand in the way of love. Jason fell in love with Kelsey and chose her as his mate. It didn't matter that she was fully human, only that she accept him as a wolf."

She nodded, refilling his glass and hers.

"My other brother, Max, has also met his mate. He lives in New Orleans now, and the woman he is going to marry has powers of her own, though they aren't lupine."

"What kind of powers?"

"Power over the weather. Her family has had this gift for centuries. Max tells me the combination of power between he and Shannon is rather…explosive."

She grinned. "Ah, so he has a woman well matched for him."

"You could say that." He watched her take a sip of wine. Didn't she realize she was torturing him with the way she licked her lips after she swallowed? His dick was twitching enough already just looking at her.

"Go on," she urged.

"My younger sister, Chantal, has just moved to San Francisco. She's been assigned to a pack there."

"Your family will not stay together?"

"No."

"That's not the pack way."

"I know. But my parents felt it important to spread the Devlin genes around the world. They have big goals, their primary one being continuation of the lupine species worldwide."

"And what about you? Were you…assigned somewhere?"

He smiled. "No, I hadn't been."

She frowned. "What's happened between us has upset your family's plans."

"Not necessarily. When my parents heard what transpired between the two of us, they made an immediate decision. I was assigned the Carpathian mountain region, the birthplace of all lupines. Now that we have an idea of what's going on here, it's imperative that the wolves are protected and nourished. When their numbers grow, we can be assured of continuity of the original bloodlines."

"This is important to you? To your family?"

"Very important. Without your ancestry, Katya, the bloodlines weaken. You are the catalyst. The beginning of it all."

"So if you and I merge…"

He smiled. "Right. We create the most powerful dynasty of lupines on Earth."

She sat back and finished her glass of wine, staring out the window at the half moon shining overhead.

Had what he said made any impact on her at all?

\* \* \* \* \*

Katya felt the pull of the moon, wishing she could strip down and run wild into the night. A desperate urge to shed more than her clothing came over her.

She wanted to rid herself of the conflicting emotions swirling through her, the need to dominate warring with the need to merge with Conner and give up some of the burden she'd carried alone for so long.

The Devlins were a powerful pack. More powerful and much more dedicated than any she'd ever come across, including her own. Her parents, the Braslieu pack, every Carpathian lupine pack she'd ever known had always been content with the status quo. To simply be allowed to exist had always been good enough.

But the Devlins thought far beyond mere existence. Their goal was to flourish, to expand, to propagate their species so their numbers could never dwindle.

She was almost embarrassed that the old ancestry had failed in realizing that they could never survive unless they fought to expand.

The Carpathian wolves hid, hoping their kind wouldn't be obliterated. They had never thought to fight against the governments, the hunters, and anyone who stood in their way.

Merely hiding and surviving wouldn't ensure their continuation.

Conner was right. They were wrong. It was time to stand up and become more powerful, not hide in the shadows and pray they weren't hunted to extinction.

Maybe she and Conner could work together on this. But only for the protection of the wolves. She was bound and determined to close off her emotions where Conner was concerned. She'd tried and failed with him, and would never open her heart. Though he intended to stay and help the pack, he wasn't the least bit interested in her except as a mate to propagate their species.

Keeping her distance from him would be the wisest thing to do. She'd never let him hurt her that way again. But how could she let her personal feelings interfere with what he hoped to accomplish here? The Devlins could be their salvation.

Besides, this was her homeland. He was a foreigner here, away from his family. Even his brother wouldn't be staying on permanently. Soon he'd be all alone, with no one to depend on. Nothing familiar, including the love of his family.

Could Katya become his family? The pack would follow their alpha, but they'd never give him their complete trust until she did.

Though she refused to sacrifice her heart for the love of the Carpathian wolves, she'd at least merge with Conner in order to help her pack. "If we do this, it has to be united."

He nodded. "I agree."

"And that means more than just you living here."

He frowned. "I'm not sure what you mean."

"It means that our bonding has to become…official."

"Official."

"What I mean is we need to marry."

The look on his face was priceless. Wide-eyed shock. She hadn't expected to surprise him, but was pleased that she'd managed to.

"You want to marry me?"

"As quickly as possible. We must merge to protect the Carpathian wolves from hunters and a government who chooses indifference in place of action."

His shock turned to a frown. "So you want to hurry this marriage along because of the wolves."

"Of course. Why else?" She'd never give him another reason than that. She'd already given too much of herself.

"Okay. How fast do your laws allow it?"

"We can have it done within a few days."

"Can you see to it?"

"I'll get Elena on it in the morning."

"Okay. Good."

Now that it had been settled, she couldn't take it back. She and Conner would marry. She fought back the panic, the fear of losing control, knowing that what she did was for her people.

She'd give Conner her cooperation and her body, but not her heart.

"We'll make beautiful babies, Katya," he whispered, picking up the end of a strand of hair and pulling it to his nose.

He inhaled and closed his eyes, murmuring something about wildflowers.

Her heart sped up, her blood racing through her veins as need began to build within her. The need to be close to Conner.

But with her body, not her heart. It was important to keep that in mind. Besides, mating with Conner would, hopefully, produce babies. She'd wanted children for as long as she could remember. Lots and lots of children.

And Conner was right. They'd make beautiful children together. She could be pregnant already and not know it. Her hand instinctively strayed to her stomach, a surge of protectiveness coursing through her.

Why not take charge of the situation? She could manipulate him as easily as he had manipulated her. "Fuck me, Conner. Now."

She stood and held out her hand, intending to take him upstairs to the bedroom. But he rose and pulled her against him, covering her mouth with his in a kiss that spoke of demand and desire.

Meeting his kiss with equal fervor, the pent-up emotions of the day spilled together in a maelstrom of frenzied passion. She craved release, and only Conner could give it to her.

His hands were everywhere at once. On her arms, her shoulders, then over her back, skimming her vertebrae, reaching for the straps of her chemise and drawing it down.

Her pants went next as he yanked the zipper down and shoved them over her hips. She stepped out of them and reached for his tie, loosening it and drawing it through his shirt, slowly pulling each inch of silk away from his neck and winding it around her hand.

His eyes shadowed, the blue-green mixing like fierce storm clouds. She reached for the buttons of his shirt, slipping each one carefully out of its hole, enjoying the quickening of his breath as she undressed him. She spread the shirt apart, splaying her hands on his chest and tangling her fingertips in the crisp hairs there. He groaned when she found his nipples and scraped them with her nails, then wound her hands down his belly, stopping at the waistband of his pants.

The hairs were soft there.

"Hurry, Katya. I'm about to lose control."

The harsh tones of his voice didn't compel her into stepping up her movements. Instead, she took her time undoing his belt and the clasp at his pants, deliberately letting her knuckles brush his erection as she painstakingly lowered the zipper.

She looked up at him, met his fiery gaze, and grinned, feeling seductive, empowered, in control of their passion. Tension coiled within Conner like a snake ready to strike, evident by the taut muscles of his abdomen as she rested her palm there.

She dropped to her knees and reached for the waistband of his pants, tugging them down until they puddled at his feet. He kicked off his shoes and stepped out of the pants, quickly shrugging out of his shirt to stand gloriously naked before her.

Her pussy quivered with the need to feel his heavy, thick cock inside her once again. But not yet. Not when his shaft was so close to her mouth and she was dying for a taste of him. She reached for it, stroking it from base to tip, then drawing the head to her mouth.

"Ah, Christ, baby," he moaned, tangling his fingers in her hair as she took him deep. "Suck me."

For once, a command she didn't mind following. She moved forward and back, taking her time in licking his essence from the tip before engulfing him once again. He jerked and tensed when she cupped his balls, squeezing the twin sacs gently as she loved him with her mouth.

"Enough!" he growled, pulling his cock away and yanking her to her feet. "I can't wait."

He drew her against him, her aching nipples scraping the hairs on his chest. She waited in breathless anticipation as he leaned slowly toward her, then took her mouth in a ravaging kiss, thrusting his tongue inside, demanding her response.

A response she was all too eager to give. She met his fervor with equal need, lifting her leg over his hip to rock her tortured sex against his shaft.

"I want you. Here, like this. Hard."

She blew out a quick breath as her heart pummeled against her ribs. He broke the kiss and turned her around, pushing her over the back of the sofa and using his knee to spread her legs apart. With relentless accuracy, his fingers roamed between her thighs, petting her moistened sex until she was on fire and whimpering.

"Fuck me Conner," she begged. "Hurry."

His breath rasped against her neck. "Oh, I'm gonna fuck you, baby. Hard and deep. You ready for this?"

"Yes!" she cried, eager to feel him buried inside her.

His cock nestled between her legs, the tip teasing her clit. She reached for his shaft, but he moved away, pressing his lips against her back, sliding his tongue along her backbone until she shivered.

Why wasn't he fucking her? What kind of game was he playing now?

"Conner."

"Mmm-hmm."

"What are you doing?" She pushed her buttocks against him, but he laughed, the deep rumble reverberating against her back.

He moved lower, his tongue trailing down the small of her back.

"Conner, what are you...oh my God!"

He'd parted her buttocks and slid his tongue along her anus.

Pleasure burst along her nerve endings, the puckered hole so sensitive she hadn't realized she could feel pleasure there. But Conner's hot, wet tongue probing the entrance was the most erotic experience she'd ever had.

"Ever put anything in your ass when you pleasure yourself, Katya?" he asked.

"N-No," she whispered.

"Do you like it when I touch you there?"

"God, yes."

"Good. I'm going to fuck you in the ass tonight."

Her belly warmed and quivered, heat settling between her legs and making her cunt spasm. The proof of her arousal seeped down her thighs, readying her pussy for his invasion. As he laved his tongue once again across her anus, she massaged her aching clit.

But then he stopped and reached for her hand, moving it away. "That's my job," he said.

"Then do it!" she commanded, surprised at the harsh tone of her own voice.

"Yes, ma'am." Conner's voice was relaxed, teasing her as if he wasn't affected at all.

But when she half turned to see his cock raging hard, the head an angry purple, she knew he wasn't oblivious to the agonizing pleasure.

"Oh I'm not taking your ass just yet. First, I want your pussy. I want to feel it squeeze my dick. Bend over, Katya."

This time he didn't take long to probe between her legs and plunge his hot cock inside her.

Wet and ready for him, she cried out when he embedded his shaft to the hilt. Her cunt squeezed him as he raked along the sensitized nerve endings in her vagina, dragging a whimpered response from her.

"So tight. So fucking perfectly made for me." He leaned over and licked her neck, sweeping her hair to the other side of her shoulder.

When he sank his teeth into the tender flesh between her neck and shoulder, his growl of possession was very clear. She climaxed, screaming as the painful pleasure of his bite mingled with the rush of sensation her orgasm had brought about.

As she rode the waves of orgasm she felt his change, her body responding in kind. Her blood boiled and she matched his howl of pleasure with one of her own.

"Stay human," he said, his voice tight, straining as he continued to pump his cock with hard thrusts.

She fought the change along with the overwhelming climax. Her knees nearly buckled as she sailed through the tumultuous waves of pleasure. Digging her fingers into the sofa cushion, she was determined to stay upright and experience more of these earth-shattering sensations.

When the tremors subsided, Conner began to move inside her, stroking her inflamed sex slowly, deliberately, until passion rose within her again.

Conner had pushed the change aside, his claws disappearing as he reached around to cup her breasts with human hands. He plucked her nipples, rocking his cock so hard against her that his balls slapped her clit, sending sparks shooting to her core.

When he removed his shaft from her cunt, she nearly cried out at the loss of fullness. But then his fingers replaced his cock, entering her, swiping at her cream and using her fluids to coat her anus.

"You're so wet when you come," he said. "So slick, a perfect lubricant."

Her cum ran from her ass down her legs as he positioned the head of his cock at the entrance to her back entrance.

"When I push in, you push back. It'll make it easier."

Emotion squeezed her chest, tightening it and making her soar with the need to please him.

"Push out, Katya. Now."

She did, and he slid past the tight muscle. She winced at the stinging pain and he stilled.

"Relax, let your body adjust."

He cupped her breasts again, lightly petting the nipples and kissing her neck and shoulders until the pain subsided. She shuddered at the incredible pleasure that replaced it.

She pushed back and more of his shaft slid inside.

"Fuck!" he cried, shoving in deeper until he was fully sheathed inside her anus.

The pain had gone, replaced by intense waves unlike anything she'd ever known. Each time with Conner was a new experience in arousal. He filled her, his thick cock stroking the sensitive nerve endings of her anus while her pussy spasmed in response to the pleasure.

She'd waited her entire life for someone like him. She'd waited to give her virginity for a reason.

She'd been waiting for him.

"Touch yourself for me, Katya. Make yourself come."

She reached for her clit, sliding her fingers between the folds of her sex and caressing the erect bud. Conner continued to stroke slowly while she built her arousal to near bursting with her hand.

"Harder," she moaned, sliding two fingers inside her wet cunt. She felt him there, the thin membrane separating her pussy from her ass allowing her to feel his thrusts within her. Her thumb found her clit and she fucked her own pussy, timing her strokes to coincide with his.

"I feel your fingers inside your cunt, baby. God, that's hot. Come for me, Katya. I want you to squeeze the juice right out of me."

She could tell he was close, and then she was lost in the feelings he evoked. Her strumming thumb drew the first sparks of orgasm, her driving fingers adding to the building tension. When Conner reared back and tunneled deeper and faster, she toppled over the edge, screaming his name as her pussy contracted and flooded her fingers with creamy cum. Spasms quaked in her ass, tightening around Conner's shaft, squeezing him.

Conner growled and came hard, shuddering against her as he filled her with hot spurts of fluid.

She collapsed over the top of the sofa, desperately trying to breathe, her legs no longer able to hold her up.

Conner withdrew slowly, swooped her into his arms and carried her upstairs, depositing her in the shower with him.

He soaped her all over, carefully washing between her legs.

Now that it was over the silence returned. Awkwardness settled between them. It was almost as if she balanced on a precipice, torn between craving him and hating him. Which way would she topple?

"Sore?" he asked, soaping her buttocks and thighs.

"A little." But she didn't care. It had been glorious, a little bit naughty and more sensual than any act she'd ever dreamed of. The intimacies she'd shared with Conner amazed her, and yet seemed as natural as breathing. She was going to have a difficult time keeping her heart out of this relationship.

Despite the way they'd come together and how he treated her outside the bedroom, there was a loneliness, a vulnerability in him that called to her heart.

As they lay in bed and he kissed her deeply before pulling her against him, she feared it was already too late.

She was in love with Conner.

# Chapter Ten

ॐ

Conner stared down at a sleeping Katya, his heart clenching with a need to protect her.

She lay on her stomach, the blanket covering her legs and buttocks but baring her perfectly shaped back to the early morning sun.

Just past dawn, the pale light cast a golden glow directly onto his woman.

His woman. His mate. The woman he—

The woman he what? Loved?

A cold dread replaced the warmth that had settled over him.

Here he was, mooning over a woman like she was the beginning and end of his existence.

What a crock.

Just because he'd mated with her didn't mean he had to love her. Mates were chosen based on urges, a primal recognition of best match.

It didn't mean love.

Hell, what would he do with a woman he loved? He already acted like half an idiot around her anyway. He'd allowed himself to get too close too fast, and let others tell him how he should treat her. She probably thought all she had to do was bitch about something he'd said or done and he'd lie down and beg forgiveness.

Weakness wasn't in his biological makeup. He'd never surrendered to a living soul before Katya.

She'd have him eating out of her hand before long. And that he couldn't allow. The alpha of the pack apologized to no one, accepted nothing less than blind loyalty.

What would her people think if they saw the way he behaved yesterday?

He'd waffled. Goddamit, he'd bent backward to let her have her way.

That wasn't going to happen again. He had things to do, and with or without her he'd see them done. If she didn't like the way he went about it, then tough shit.

She'd just have to learn to accept the fact that he made all the decisions now.

Today's agenda was a big one. He planned to march into the land and game ministry's office and demand better protection for the Carpathian wolves.

To think he'd actually thought about discussing the situation with Katya.

He was pussy-whipped, all right.

But not for long. He stepped into the bathroom and dressed quickly, then tiptoed out of the room so he wouldn't wake her.

With a new determination in mind, he went in search of Noah, finding him and Elena sharing coffee in the kitchen.

He turned and grinned. "Have a good evening?"

That question didn't deserve an answer. "We're going to the ministry this morning."

Noah looked to Elena, then back at Conner. "Taking Katya with you?"

"Nope." He downed the hot brew in two gulps, then poured himself another. Christ they made strong coffee here. "I'm taking you with me."

When Noah didn't answer, Conner asked, "You got a problem with that?"

Noah shrugged and set down his cup. "I don't have a problem with anything. I'll go get ready."

But as he walked past, Noah shook his head and clapped him on the shoulder. "You're the one who's going to have a problem, bro. From the frying pan into the fire, as Mom always says."

Just once, Conner would love to knock that smirk right off Noah's face.

* * * * *

"Gone? What do you mean he's gone?"

Elena winced at the rising tone of Katya's voice. "He left with Noah. Something about going to the ministry this morning."

He'd done it to her again. Unbelievable. Had she dreamed last night? His apology, the way he'd said he would involve her in everything from now on?

She must have, because this morning he was back to the way he'd been yesterday. Doing things on his own, without once seeking her counsel.

"Fucking asshole dog. I hope he slips in shit and has to eat it. I hope his dick rots and falls off from disease."

Elena winced. "I'm sorry, cousin. I thought things would improve."

"Yes, well, we were both wrong, then." Unable to face the people milling about the castle, she headed up to her room, content to pace in front of the window by herself, plotting ways to do away with Conner.

No that she could, or even would, but visualizing his gruesome demise made her feel somewhat better. And she did need an outlet for her profound anger.

Better mental than physical. She might not be his match, strength-wise, but she could do some serious damage to his nearly perfect body before he could take her down.

She'd just about mentally bled him to death when she saw him and Noah approach through the gates. Determined not to seek him out, she waited, fuming and pacing. It didn't take him long to open the bedroom door, slamming it hard behind him.

She refused to turn around and look at him, instead focusing on the mocking bright sunlight of the beautiful day.

But as soon as he started spouting off his pompous, arrogant statements about how he was in charge of things, she was going to kick his ass.

"Your government is run by the most provincial, backward, unyielding sons of bitches I've ever had the displeasure to meet."

Tell her something she didn't know. Oh, wait, if he'd bothered to consult her, she would have told him that. So he wasted his time this morning.

Good. She didn't even try to hide her smirk, but she refused to speak to him.

"I went to talk to them about the laws, about beefing up protection for the wolves in the Carpathians. I quoted statistics, realties versus fallacies, every bit of logical, documented information I had. You know what they said?"

"Yes."

"Huh?"

She turned then. "I said yes. I know what they said. They said they were sorry, but the laws would remain as they always had. After all, one does not change something as important as environment and ecology overnight. These things take time. Study. More facts are needed before they can proceed with more security for the Carpathian wolves."

His jaw dropped. "You just quoted the man verbatim."

"Yes." Disgusted, she turned and faced the window again.

"How did you know?"

She squeezed her eyes shut, forcing herself to remain calm. *Don't even answer him, Katya. He is not worth your anger.*

"Katya. What's wrong?"

She bit her lip until it bled. She would not answer him.

When he reached for her, wrapping his fingers around her upper arms, she tensed, partially shifted, growling and clawing at him.

Conner jumped back, his eyes wide. "What the fuck is wrong with you?"

She shifted back to fully human, refusing to feel guilty for the blood seeping from the wound on the back of his hand.

He was lucky he still had two balls.

"Katya, why did you attack?"

"Get out, Conner. Before I do something I won't regret."

He went silent for a moment, and she'd actually thought he might leave. But he didn't.

"Oh, I get it. You're pissed because I went to the ministry without you."

"And they said you were stupid."

"Huh? Who said I was stupid?"

She rolled her eyes and turned to face him. "You promised me last night that you would consult me."

He looked past her, out the window, then met her gaze. "I did what I needed to do. I won't apologize for it again."

"So you decided that maybe last night's apology was premature. That maybe you showed weakness by allowing the female alpha to bend you to her will. You suffered some kind of testosterone meltdown and decided to teach me a lesson. Let me know when I'm getting close to the truth."

Close? Fuck, she'd hit the nail right on the head. Her insight was uncanny. And the woman was one vicious lupine when she was pissed off.

"So how did it work for you, Conner? Oh, that's right, it didn't."

"You need to understand the way it's supposed to work, Katya. I'm the alpha. I'm supposed to make all the decisions, and you're supposed to follow along."

"Supposed to? I don't think so. The Braslieu pack has had a female alpha leading them since my father died. So much for tradition. They may hold onto some of the old ways, but they can bend in others. Perhaps you should consider the same."

"I won't bend in this."

"Then you'll be truly alone, because I won't yield to you and become some simpering, empty-headed mate that you only keep around to fuck. If that's what you want, go find someone else, because our association will end right now."

"There can't be two alphas."

She laughed. "There already are. And with you and me at odds, how long do you think it will take before my people realize that they gain nothing by having you as their leader, and everything by having me?"

His eyes narrowed, his body stance taut with tension. "Don't threaten me, Katya."

"Then don't insult me by expecting me to be something I'm not, Conner."

She heard the growl, low and menacing, but refused to budge. Yes, he could harm her physically, but she didn't fear him. He'd never hurt her, no matter how angry she made him.

Though she wasn't the type to lash out physically, either, and she had.

Conner obviously brought out the worst in her.

"I'd say we've reached an impasse," she offered. "Please leave my room and don't come back."

"Gladly." He turned on his heel and in two long strides was gone.

Katya exhaled and sat on the bed, her limbs trembling.

Whether from fear, misery or outright anger, she couldn't tell.

But one thing was certain.

Neither of them had won that skirmish.

And she feared a war was coming.

* * * * *

"You did it again? Holy Christ, Conner, are you a glutton for punishment?"

Conner did his best to ignore Noah. Instead, he kept his focus on the paperwork on Katya's desk, determined to figure out an angle that would work on the ministry.

"Elena told me what happened yesterday."

"Remind me to have Elena sent to the far border of Braslieu land. She talks too much."

"She's Katya's cousin, for God's sake. Don't you think the two of them speak? She's also Katya's beta and you know that gives her certain rights."

Conner looked up at his brother. "Just whose side are you on here, bro? Mine, or Katya's?"

"Yours, of course, except you're doing it all wrong."

"I took advice from you once. Unsolicited. Notice how I'm not soliciting it now?"

"I really think you should—"

"Look," Conner said, rising from the chair and sliding the file folder shut. "I've taken all the "you shoulds" that I can handle. I'm not going to play meek puppy dog to placate the princess. She's going to have to learn to adapt to change, just like everyone else around here."

"You're going to lose her, Con."

Conner refused to be swayed by his brother's statement. "If I do, I do. There's plenty of pussy around here." But even that statement left him feeling hollow and empty.

Noah shook his head. "Now you sound like me. And that's not a good thing. Because you aren't anything like me."

"Thank God."

"Keep it up, Con," Noah said, heading for the door. "In record time, just about everyone here will be wishing you'd never set foot on Braslieu land. Including me."

Conner winced at the slam of the heavy door.

The silence wasn't as comforting as he'd hoped. The sun had long since departed, leaving the nearly full moon tormenting him through the window.

The pull grew stronger, as did his need.

For Katya.

He dropped his head into his hands and wished he was anywhere but here. It sure as hell seemed like he couldn't win, no matter what he did.

"What the fuck is wrong with wanting to be an alpha?"

The moon offered no response.

A silvery cloud sailed across the three quarter moon, obliterating its light. Hell, even the moon had turned its back on him.

He'd never felt more alone in his life. Or more like a failure. He'd always been taught to handle those around him who wanted to dominate him. There was only room for one alpha in a pack, and he was alpha of this one. Not a very good one, though.

And for the life of him, he didn't know what to do now. Nor did he have anyone to talk to about it. Not even Noah. Noah and he didn't think the same way about things. They'd always been sun and moon, night and day. Opposites in so many ways, especially their philosophies. Funny, though, he'd expected Noah to stand behind him in this.

"I guess I'm just goddamned wrong about everything."

"About goddamned time you figured that out, brother dear."

He lifted his head, shocked at the voice he hadn't expected to hear, especially in person.

Chantal.

"What are you doing here?"

She waltzed in looking fresh and beautiful as usual, her hair pulled back in a ponytail and looking like she just walked off the pages of a glossy fashion magazine.

"Thanks so much for the welcome." She set her briefcase down and came over to the desk to kiss his cheek. "You're in deep trouble."

"Who says?"

"Noah, for one. And he's not one to call for help. And he sure as hell would never think to call me in unless it was a dire emergency."

"There's no emergency."

Chantal crossed her arms. "Really? And how's Katya? How much progress have you made with her and your current situation?"

He groaned. "Shit."

"Going that well, huh?"

"The last thing I need is another pain in the ass alpha female in the mix."

"Oh, but there's a difference. I'm not the pain in the ass alpha female you're in love with."

He glared at her. "Who said I was in love with Katya?"

"I did."

"You don't even know her."

"I don't have to. I know you. The fact you've completely alienated her can mean only one thing. She's gotten under your skin and you have no idea how to handle her. Because she isn't your usual piece of fluff that you fuck, and she isn't a part of the business that you can just deal with as you see fit."

Sometimes he really hated Chantal's insights. "So?"

Her grin brightened up the gloom in the office. "So I'm here to rescue you. Aren't you just the luckiest sonofabitch on the face of the Earth?"

* * * * *

Katya may loathe Conner Devlin right now, but she was absolutely crazy in love with his sister, Chantal.

What complete opposites. Yes, Chantal was definitely an alpha female, but she had emotions. And she understood Katya's plight.

What was even better, she agreed with her complaints about Conner.

"Yes, my brother is a huge pain in the ass. You're very wise to discover that so quickly in the game. That says a lot about your intellect, Katya. Most people don't figure that out until after he's been around a while."

They sat at the kitchen table drinking coffee and trading stories about Conner.

Thought Katya's experience with him had been limited, she'd learned a lot about him in a short period of time. Though she hadn't shared quite everything with Chantal. Namely, the passion that she'd experienced with Conner.

She doubted Chantal would want to hear those details.

"I can't believe you've run this huge pack all these years," Chantal said. "That must have been quite a burden for you."

"I could have continued to handle things myself."

"Having help isn't admitting failure, Katya."

She shrugged.

"Anyway, let's get down to business. Tell me exactly what's going on with Conner."

"He's a pain in my ass."

Chantal laughed. "Understandable. I remember when Noah and Conner were teens. Lord did they drive my mother crazy. I just sat there with the halo over my head while they got in trouble."

Katya could well envision the family dynamics of the Devlins. She wished she could have seen Conner grow up. "I'll bet Conner was a troublemaker even then."

Rolling her eyes dramatically, Chantal said, "Honey, you have no idea."

She'd never felt this comfortable so quickly with another person. Chantal had breezed in unapologetically and informed her she was here to help. Having experience with international law would also assist them with the ministry. At least that was the reason Chantal gave for showing up here.

But she got the idea that Conner's sister had come for another reason entirely, despite her claims to be here to help the Carpathian cause.

"Your brother is stubborn."

"Mmm-hmm," Chantal answered, sipping her coffee.

"And unreasonable."

"Yes."

"He refuses to acknowledge my rights."

"Typical."

"He treats me like a woman."

"The bastard."

Katya laughed, realizing how ridiculous that sounded. With a resigned sigh, she added, "And I'm in love with him."

"I'm so sorry to hear that, honey," Chantal said, then grinned.

"How do I handle him? I feel like if I bow to his dominance, I lose a part of myself."

"You don't have to give up any of yourself to love someone. If that person loves you, then there's always a compromise."

She shook her head. "I can see no way to compromise. He simply wishes to take over and do things his way without including me."

"Then you have to keep reminding him to include you."

She lifted her chin. "I shouldn't have to remind him. He should know what to do."

Chantal arched a brow. "Now who's being the stubborn alpha?"

It hadn't occurred to her until Chantal said the words. "You know, you're absolutely right. I'm as bad as he is."

Laughing, Chantal clasped her hand and squeezed. "The great thing about women is that we can admit our flaws. Men, on the other hand…"

"Very true. We do need to walk more than halfway to meet them in the middle, don't we?"

"With my brother, yeah, I'm afraid so. But if it's any comfort, I believe he's in love with you."

Katya snorted. "That's highly unlikely. He hates me. He thinks I deliberately seduced him to take him as my mate. Which, by the way, I didn't. I had…a rough night that night. Then I drank too much brandy to numb the shock, and one thing led to another."

Chantal held up her hand. "You don't need to explain to me. I believe you. And trust me. I know Conner. If he didn't love you, I wouldn't still be here. He'd have railed and complained and done whatever necessary to get me on a plane out of here as fast as possible. The last thing he'd want is my help."

"And?"

"He asked me to stay. To help him figure a way that he could work things out with you."

She found that hard to believe, and was irritated at the sense of hope she felt at Chantal's statement. "He told you this?"

"Not in so many words, but that was the gist of our conversation. Trust me, Katya, he's got it bad for you. All you have to do now is take the upper hand, and move in for the kill."

Yes, she liked Chantal more and more every minute she spent with Conner's cunning sister. She'd given Katya hope that maybe her feelings for Conner weren't unfounded. Perhaps their relationship wasn't completely doomed to failure.

If she could give a little, maybe Conner would too.

# Chapter Eleven

ഇ

"Don't you have business to attend to in San Francisco?"

For three days Conner had dealt with Chantal underfoot, picking away at him until he had no choice but to sit down and listen to her harp about his treatment of Katya. He tapped his fingers on the desk and waited.

"Of course I have business in San Francisco. Well, moving in, anyway. The job doesn't start for another few weeks, so until then I'm all yours."

He looked to the heavens for intervention. "Oh, joy. I'm sure Mom and Dad would love to see you."

"Quit evading the issue. Pull your head out of your ass and make some headway with Katya."

"Katya is a stubborn, unreasonable pain in the ass."

Chantal smirked. "Funny, she said the same thing about you."

"That figures." Lord, save him from his own family. "I'm doing fine."

"You are not. You've made no progress at all with the ministry, you can't even get your foot in the door and Katya won't speak to you. Aren't you two mated or something?"

"Yes." Not that anyone could tell. The cold castle had become even more frigid over the last few days.

"I haven't seen the two of you occupy the same room, let alone a bedroom, since I came here."

"She's being obstinate."

Arching her brows, Chantal said, "So are you. Meet her halfway, Conner. Otherwise you're wasting your time here. Her people won't follow you if she doesn't."

Tired of hearing this same speech from his brother and sister, he said, "Yeah, they will. I'm alpha. They have no choice."

"Haven't you ever seen another male take over a pack?"

"Yeah. But it won't happen here. I'm much stronger than any of their males."

"Famous last words." Chantal examined one long, red fingernail. "I'll miss you when they beat you to a bloody pulp in their takeover."

"Thanks for the vote of confidence."

She stood and stretched, then headed to the window. "Even now, they're plotting against you."

"You watch too much television."

"I'm watching out the window, you idiot. There are at least a dozen males huddled together, and occasionally glancing up here at the office. Do you think they're planning a surprise birthday party for you? Come on, Con. They see how unhappy Katya is. They're worried about the future of their pack. They don't see you as a leader. The tension around this place is thick. Everyone's worried about their future. If you can't gain Katya's cooperation and trust, how will you ever gain theirs?"

Fuck. He didn't need this. He'd already apologized once. He goddamn well wasn't going to do it again.

"You might be right. I do need her. For cooperative reasons only."

"Of course."

She didn't believe him, judging by the smirk she tried unsuccessfully to hide. He didn't really care. He'd do what he had to do to gain Katya's assistance in the planning efforts for the wolves, but that was it. If she wanted him to touch her again, *she'd* damn well have to get on her knees and beg, because he was no woman's puppy dog.

Apologizing to her the first time had been a critical error on his part. It wouldn't happen again. He could live without his mate's love. What the fuck would he do with love anyway? It just caused problems and he had enough problems to deal with.

"I'll go talk to her."

Chantal crossed her arms and graced him with a satisfied smile. "Good."

But on his terms, not hers. He stood and headed for the door. No time like the present to get the unpleasant business out of the way.

"She's in love with you, you know."

He stopped and turned. "No, she's not."

"Yeah, she is."

"Did she tell you that?"

"I'm not at liberty to say."

"What the fuck does that mean?"

"That means I'm not telling you how I know. I just know."

He narrowed his gaze on his sharply cunning sister. "You made it up."

"If you say so."

Damn Chantal for putting that thought in his head. Did Katya love him? How could she possibly have any feelings for him at all, other than hatred? He'd pushed her away by not including her in pack business, not once, but twice. He'd accused her of deliberately entrapping him into a mate bond. It wouldn't make any sense for her to be in love with him.

"Don't screw with me, Chantal. I need to know."

His sister shrugged. "Then you're asking the wrong person. Go ask Katya how she feels."

"No fucking way."

"Your choice, Con. Good luck. I'm going to go soak in the tub." She walked past him and stopped, throwing her arms around him for a quick hug. Just as quickly, she pulled away and said, "Not many of us are fortunate enough to find someone willing to put up with us. I'd say you're one of the lucky ones. What you choose to do with that knowledge is up to you, but if you screw up again, you're never going to get another chance."

She turned and walked out of the office, leaving him standing there more confused than ever.

How far would Chantal go to placate Katya? His sister would never do anything to hurt him that much he knew for certain. Their family was tight and always honest with each other. Brutally honest.

If he took what his sister said as truth, then the game changed considerably. Or maybe it wasn't a game at all, and he had to quit looking like it as some kind of challenge he had to win.

Shaking his head, he went in search of Katya, formulating what he was going to say when he found her. She was nowhere to be found in the castle. Elena told him she'd gone outside to enjoy the day. It was unseasonably warm and she said Katya liked to take a swim in the heated pools. Armed with directions to the water, he headed outside and into the woods.

God, how long had it been since he'd shifted and run wild? It seemed like that was a distant part of his past, never to be repeated again. Would he ever have that kind of freedom again?

The need grew stronger as he forged deeper into the forest. Not paying the slightest bit of attention to the fallen logs and branches, he used his senses to step over anything blocking his path.

The air cooled considerably, the sunlight partially blocked by the heavy branches overhead. Conner stopped and inhaled, closing his eyes when he picked up Katya's scent.

He was amazingly in sync with her, even though they were at odds. Sucking in a brain-clearing whiff of air, he frowned when he realized the air carried the musk of arousal.

Her arousal. Distinct, her sweet perfume entered his senses and shot straight between his legs, readying his cock for mating.

So enticing, he'd follow her scent anywhere.

But wait. Why the hell was she aroused when she wasn't with him? Fury rolled through him and a fierce possessiveness kicked in.

Godammit! Katya was *his* mate. *His* woman. No other man was allowed to touch her.

If she was with someone else, he'd kill the guy. Taking more determined steps, he followed her scent, churning branches in his way like a bear on a rampage.

Yeah, he was on a fucking rampage, all right. God help the man who touched her because he wouldn't be able to control himself.

Her scent grew stronger as he spotted a clearing ahead, charging in that direction until he pushed through the thick branches and stopped.

The vision before him wasn't what he'd expected to see at all.

Katya was alone, naked, lying on the banks of a steamy pool of water, her fingers roaming between her legs. Her eyes were shut, feet flat on the ground, knees bent, the position offering him a perfect view of her pussy. Moisture glistened around the swollen lips, seeping down the crack of her ass.

When she moaned he hardened fully, fighting back a desperate urge to dive between her legs and lick up all that cream until she cried out, her screams echoing through the forest.

Would she scramble away if he approached her? God, he hated disturbing the erotic scene in front of him. Maybe he could linger quietly for a while and just watch. Then again, with Katya's lupine senses, she'd figure out soon enough that he was there.

Deciding to meet her on equal ground, he pulled off his jacket and shirt and shed his jeans and boots, then stepped out of the woods and onto the soft grass.

He'd no more cleared the trees than she stopped and opened her eyes, staring directly at him. But rather than jumping to her feet and reaching for her clothes, she shifted up on her elbows and watched him approach, her face devoid of expression. He had no idea whether she was happy or irritated to see him.

His desire was quite evident, hardening further when her gaze focused on his erection. He sat down next to her on the grassy bank.

"Still angry at me?"

"Fiercely."

Shit. Okay, maybe a neutral conversation first, just to break the ice between them a little. "Taking a swim?"

Her lips curled in a sardonic smile. "No, I was masturbating."

He laughed. "So I noticed. Damn, Katya. That's hot."

"Glad you thought so. Then again, I *had* planned to do it alone."

That was probably his signal to get up and leave. The problem was he didn't want her doing it alone. He didn't want to do it alone. His cock belonged in her pussy. Today, tomorrow, forever. It was time to force thoughts of sex away and talk to Katya about their problems.

"Katya, we need to talk."

She tilted her head to the side, looked him up and down, and shook her head. "I don't think so."

He knew she'd make this difficult. "Look, I know you don't want to talk about us, but we have to."

"You don't understand, Conner. You're right. We do need to talk. About a lot of things. But not right now. You walked in on me when I was close to coming. So like it or not, you need to take care of my immediate problem. The rest of it we'll talk about later. Right now I'm horny as hell, my cunt aches and I need you inside me. I need to come."

Holy shit. Maybe they were closer to a consensus than he thought.

* * * * *

Katya chewed her bottom lip and waited for Conner's response.

Suggesting he make love to her hadn't been on the top of her list when she'd seen him walking toward her, naked and aroused. She should have stood and ordered him to leave her alone so she could have her privacy. Her visions while masturbating had been of him doing exactly what he'd done — show up in the forest naked and erect, ready to fuck her like she needed to be fucked.

She realized that now was the time to either move their relationship forward, or end it completely. They may be at odds in many areas, but sex wasn't one of them. And that was a starting point to breach the distance between them.

"Well?" she asked, impatient for his response.

His lips curved upward. "I was at a loss for words."

"Find them yet?" She pulled her knees to her chest and wrapped her arms around them. If he said no, she'd be mortified. But then she'd know that Chantal was wrong. That he didn't care for her at all.

He turned and wrapped his palm around the back of her neck, pulling her mouth to his. Before their lips touched, he said, "I want you, Katya. So much that it hurts. I'll always want you."

She sighed her relief into his open mouth, wrapping her arms around his back and pressing her breasts against his chest.

They both moved to their knees, their bodies aligned breasts to chest, belly to belly and sex to sex. His chest hairs tickled her breasts, teasing her nipples to sharp points. She shifted from side to side, creating her own pleasure by rubbing the aroused buds against the hard muscles of his chest.

He groaned and she felt the vibration against her breasts. His cock jutted up between them and she rocked against it, its heat burning her lower belly.

She needed his cock inside her. Right now. Thoughts of making love with him had permeated her every thought the past couple of days. Despite her anger and frustration with him, her desire for him hadn't diminished. In fact, it had grown stronger.

Was it possible to love and want someone desperately while still angry as hell at them?

"Fuck me, Conner. And hurry," she urged, moving back to lie on the grass. She spread her legs while he kneeled there and watched, stroking his shaft. Never had she felt so wanton, so free. Maybe it was being outside, their natural element, but she wanted him to see how much she desired him.

Opening her legs, she showed him her need, sliding her hand over her belly to pet her sex.

His gaze flamed hot, burning her, spurring her on to be even more adventurous. She slipped two fingers into her wet pussy, thrusting in and out slowly, then withdrew them and brought her fingers to her mouth to taste her own desire.

"Fuck, Katya. That's so goddamn erotic." His movements increased as he stroked his shaft hard and fast from base to tip. Creamy drops spilled from the tip of his penis, and he swirled his thumb over the liquid.

Her nostrils flared, taking in the musky scent of him, desperate to feel the jetting of that hot seed deep inside her with a need that was borne of primal urges and a frantic sense of urgency.

His scent made her crazy, drove her to dig deep inside herself and find the wild part of her that she'd suppressed for so many years.

"I can smell you," he said. "Hot, musky. You bring out the beast in me, Katya. Make yourself come for me."

At this point it was highly unlikely she could hold back anyway. One or two more strokes and she'd —

A scream tore from her throat, her hips bucking off the soft grass as her climax rushed over her in a tidal wave so powerful it made her lightheaded. She kept her gaze on Conner's face as she sailed into oblivion, somehow finding the eye contact more stimulating than she ever thought possible. She was coming, and he was watching her.

"Oh yeah," Conner growled, moving toward her and dropping down between her legs to bury his head at her sex. The spasms of her orgasm had not yet subsided when he licked her cream in slow, soft laps of his tongue, taking in the juices that poured from her and driving her near mad in the process.

Despite her first rip-roaring orgasm, she was recharged by his devouring mouth, unable to even catch her breath between her self-induced orgasm and the next one that Conner brought her to.

She tangled her fingers in his hair and soared over the edge again, thrusting her sex against his greedy mouth. He held onto her hips and devoured her juices until she collapsed, exhausted and unable to even speak.

"Oh, we haven't even begun, Katya," Conner rumbled, lifting and turning her over to position her on her hands and knees.

"I love taking you like this," he said, his voice tight with need as he probed between her legs and thrust hard and deep inside her cunt.

She whimpered, feeling that now-familiar fullness and shocked to discover that she did, indeed, still have more desire to slake. With Conner it only took seconds for her drive to begin anew, seconds for him to take her the point that she lost her sanity and wanted only to rush over that blissful edge again.

"Fuck me, Katya. Back that sweet ass against me and fuck me hard."

Unable to help the wolf's emergence, she embraced the wildness within her and growled at her mate, thrusting her ass back against his pelvis and squeezing his cock with the muscles of her cunt.

His claws emerged, the stinging sharp pain of them digging into the flesh of her hips. But Katya did not object. She welcomed the savage thrust against her, the beast within him roaring to life. He moved with the wildness that lived within her, his balls slapping her clit and bringing her closer and closer to orgasm.

The heat of the day bore down on their skin, sweat pouring from their bodies and mixing with the wetness of their lust.

Their coupling was primal, urgent, like the wolves that lived inside them. Her skin prickled as the hair thickened on her arms and back, her jaw feeling as if it were splitting open as her face began to change.

That was all she would allow, feeling more vulnerable in her animal state than she ever did as a human. She shouldn't feel that way, since as a wolf she was much stronger, but maintaining her humanity, even in something as raw and primal as sex, was important.

Conner followed her lead and only partially transformed, enough so she could feel his blood boiling with the change from human to lupine. His cock grew hotter, thicker, filling her walls and scraping the sensitive tissues inside her until she cried out from the pleasure.

The fever of the moment added to Katya's excitement, notching up her desire until she whimpered like an animal in heat.

She *was* like an animal in heat and reveled in her power over lesser beasts.

"Harder," she urged, bucking against Conner's cock, needing him deeper inside her. He obliged by pistoning so deeply she felt his thrusts in her womb.

And then she splintered apart, tilting her head up and howling as her climax tore through her.

Conner went with her, his wolf cry echoing through the empty forest, his hot cum jetting into her cunt. Their feral growls mixed in a song as sweet as any she'd ever heard. They collapsed onto the grassy bank, their bodies returning to human form while they found normal breathing again.

She lay there and stared at him, mesmerized by the beauty and rugged angles of his face. Dark stubble lined his jaw and she reached out to feel its scrape against her palm, not at all surprised to feel the tingle of excitement spark within her.

They were completely untamed together. But as wild as their lovemaking had been, it didn't begin to solve their other problems. Problems that seemed insurmountable.

He had sought her out to talk. It was time to find out what he had come to say.

"You wanted to talk to me?"

He smiled. "I'd rather have sex again."

"But we're not going to. Now talk to me. That is why you came here."

"Yeah, I did come here to talk. That is, until I found this mirage in the clearing. A wild thing with her legs spread as if she was waiting for me."

Katya's lips curled upward. "I was waiting for you. In a way. But I never expected you to show up just as I slid my hand between my legs."

He inhaled deeply and caressed the tip of one nipple. "Just thinking about the way I found you spread-eagled on the grass has my cock getting hard again."

Katya looked at it and shook her head.

"Talk first. Sex later."

He sat up and ran his fingers through his hair. "I've always taken charge in business. I'm a leader. An alpha. It's my way or nothing."

She leaned up on her elbows. "So I noticed."

"But I've realized that I'm beating my head against a stone wall trying to do this myself. And I've got enough of my family ganging up on me to open my eyes and realize how much I need help."

Why couldn't he have figured that out without his brother and sister pointing it out to him? Then again, she was rather fond of this hard-headed alpha. Perhaps his stubbornness could be beneficial. He certainly would never back down under a challenge, that much was certain.

"I can help you, Conner, if you'd only let me. Keep in mind that I have run this territory since my parents died. I know what works and what doesn't."

One corner of his mouth lifted. "So what you're saying is I'm probably already doing things you've already done."

"I didn't say it."

"You don't have to. This is never going to be easy for me, Katya. But I'm willing to give it a try. I need your help. I can't, and frankly, I don't want to do this alone."

His admission was all she needed to hear. She sat up, reached for his face and kissed him tenderly, pouring her heart out to him. "You don't have to do it alone."

"I've missed you," he mumbled against her mouth, licking her bottom lip and tugging at it with his teeth.

She laughed at the same time her body flamed to life once again. "I've missed you, too."

He drew circles around her nipples, plucking the buds when they drew into hardened points and making her forget what they were talking about.

"We should get started on business," he suggested, but one look told her that business as the last thing on his mind.

"Later. I need your cock in me again. We'll talk business when we get back to the castle."

* * * * *

True to his word, Conner had asked for her help. And she'd given it, realizing that the two of them together were a powerful force. They'd stormed into the ministry and bullied them into placing a temporary halt to all hunting of wolves until the Devlins could set up the foundation.

"We need to get married, and fast," Conner said, glancing over at her while they sat at the huge dining table with Noah, Chantal, Elena and a handful of the Carpathian shifters.

"I know. The ministry will never recognize you until we are married. You and I must be married for three years before you can attain Romanian citizenship."

"But once we're married they will at least recognize me as having a stake in what happens here."

Katya nodded. "True. You can placate them with money and promises of tourism and good public relations for a short period of time, but eventually the hunter coalitions and the farmers will have their way again, and wolves will be hunted as they always have. Besides, even if our country's ministry defends the rights of the wolves, as soon as the lupines cross the borders into Slovakia or Ukraine they are no longer protected by Romanian law."

"Open hunting season," Elena said, wrinkling her nose. "And we're nearing that time of year. Those of us who are shifters can watch where we roam, but we cannot keep the pure wolves from crossing borders. Even when we change, we operate on primal instinct rather than human sense. If we roam over the borders, we will be subject to being shot by hunters, too."

Conner nodded. "That's what we have to change. The refuge will help. Crews should be arriving any day to erect the walls keeping the wolves within the Romanian borders."

"But that will only do so much good," Katya said. "A wolf that does not want to be contained will not be. And the wild ones, even the ancient shifters, believe that all the land of the Carpathian mountain range is theirs to wander. They don't recognize the borders of countries."

"Then we have to work harder to convince the bordering nations to limit their hunting and protect the wolves."

Conner knew this wasn't going to happen overnight. Change of this magnitude could take years, especially when dealing with something as delicate as foreign policy.

But marrying Katya and merging the Devlins with the Braslieus would bring about more power. And frankly, no matter what the nation's politics, money talked.

But would they be able to offer enough to thwart the hunting lobbies?

"We have a lot to do. Let's get married tomorrow."

Katya's eyes widened, then she nodded. "Okay. I will make arrangements for the mayor to come to the castle and say the vows."

His mother was going to kill him for getting married without her being present, but Conner figured after they had things under control he'd drag Katya to Boston and do the big family wedding his mother had always wanted.

"I am sorry we have to rush through this and your parents cannot be here with us," she said after most of the people had left.

"Me, too. Mom's going to kick my ass for doing this without her. You wouldn't want to call her and break the news to her for me, would you?" he asked, looking to Chantal.

Chantal shook her head. "Are you insane? I don't want to be the one to face Mom's wrath. You know how mothers get about their children getting married. As it is you'll probably be disowned and stricken from the will."

Noah snorted. Conner glared. Katya looked to all of them with a worried expression. "We could always wait and invite your parents out for the wedding. What can a few weeks matter?"

Conner kissed the top of her head and wrapped his arm around her. "Mom's going to love you, Little Miss Proper. But no. I want to be married as soon as possible."

"Because of the work we have to do with the ministry?"

He knew what she was asking, but he'd be damned if he was ready to admit it out loud. He was still trying to get used to the idea himself. "I want you pregnant."

"That may have already happened, as you well know," she said, her cheeks turning a sexy pink.

He grinned. "Sooner rather than later suits me just fine." The thought of her carrying his child filled him with awe, and he realized he really did want Katya pregnant. Very soon.

Christ, how his life had changed.

Chantal coughed, but he ignored her. If he was going to give Katya a goddamn declaration of love, he sure as hell wasn't going to do it in front of witnesses.

Love. Did he really love her? Did he even know what it meant to love someone? Then again, he'd changed in the short time he'd been here. Whereas before he'd never consulted anyone outside the family, now he'd become dependent on Katya's counsel. The past few days they'd spent every moment together, from plotting out their next move over coffee and breakfast each morning to breathing fire in the ministry's office, playing off each other's strengths as if they'd been partnered for years instead of only a week.

Katya was fierce, tenacious, refusing to back down and never afraid to voice her opinion, especially to him.

They argued with each other well into the night, where their passion for the wolves turned to passion for each other.

Could he have found a better mate than Katya? He doubted it. She really was his destiny. She was everything he'd ever wanted in a lover, a mate, even a business partner.

Damn, he was one lucky man.

"Before you devour the woman on the dining room table, I'm getting out of here," Chantal said.

"Right behind you," Noah added, winking at Conner and following his sister.

"I thought they'd never leave." He picked up her hand, brushing his lips over each knuckle, then turning her hand over to lick her palm.

Katya shivered, her dark eyes glazing over with a passion that he would never tire of seeing.

"Are you quite sure about marrying me?" she asked.

He read the uncertainty in her voice. "I don't say what I don't mean. I knew someday I'd be required to seek out a mate, to find a pack's alpha female and create a dynasty. How damn lucky I am to find out it was you."

"There are things you need to know about the ceremony. Rituals that are required."

Oh, God. Now that kind of stuff he didn't want to hear about. Clothes and flowers and stand here and do this and that. "Baby, if it's tradition, we'll do it. You take care of that part, okay?"

"But I think you need to know that after the wedding ceremony…"

Once again he cut her off. "The only thing I'm interested in after the ceremony is having you alone."

"That's what I'm talking about. It's customary for—"

This time he silenced her with a kiss. When he pulled back her cheeks were flushed. "Go make your arrangements. I don't need to approve every detail of the wedding. I'll be there, we'll get married. The rest will happen according to your customs and we'll take it one step at a time."

She blushed and stood. "All right. I have a lot to do to prepare for the wedding."

"Will I see you in bed tonight?"

She leaned up on her toes and kissed him softly, sliding her tongue inside his mouth and tantalizing him with a heated promise. "Of course you will. And tonight, I get to be alpha and ravage you from on top."

He couldn't think of a better way to submit to his woman.

And tomorrow, she'd be his wife.

He shook his head and pondered his own happiness. Life was sure strange. In the blink of an eye, everything changed.

# Chapter Twelve

ℰℴ

Katya undressed and ran out into the forest, letting the wolf take over. Her body burned with the adjustment in anatomy, but she welcomed the pain, hoping it would clear her head.

So many times the past few days she wanted to tell Conner how she felt about him, but something stopped her.

She raced to the top of the tallest hill on Braslieu land, knowing her boundaries, retaining just enough of her humanity to keep her senses.

The moon was nearly full as it rose over the tallest mountain peak. She closed her eyes and breathed in its power, hoping for the strength to see her through the next step of her life journey.

Conner.

She loved him.

She hadn't loved anyone since her parents died, fearing if she lost another that she loved, she'd never survive it. Instead, she had kept her heart encased in a wall of stone, impervious to feeling.

Until Conner, who'd stormed in and broken down that wall as if were nothing but the weakest wall of sand.

Hearing from Chantal that Conner was in love with her gave her conflicting feelings of euphoria and fear. Who wouldn't want a man to love her? But love meant the possibility of loss, and she didn't think she could take it if something happened to him. Could she live with him, sleep with him every night, share her body with him but still keep her heart removed?

She wasn't certain she was capable of that. And what of children? More people to love, more potential for loss?

The moon provided no answers to the pain in her heart.

As always, she would do what she had to do and hope she never had to face that kind of loss again.

\* \* \* \* \*

"For Christ's sake, Con, breathe."

Conner swallowed and inhaled deeply, glaring at Noah. "I *am* breathing, dammit!"

He was getting married in an hour. An hour. Married. He still had a hard time wrapping his head around this whirlwind that had been his life lately.

And now he was dressed in Romanian garb, following their custom. Tight black pants and a crisp white shirt. He felt like a pirate, but what the hell.

"All you need is a broadsword, an eye patch and maybe an earring and you'll be all set to rape and pillage."

"Fuck off, Noah."

Noah just laughed and led the way to the small chapel contained within the castle. An arched doorway was decorated with white flowers. He didn't even know what they were or how they got there, but he assumed the people of Braslieu had spent the evening setting up decorations in the chapel.

A white linen carpet lined the short walkway from the entryway to the altar, where he and Noah waited. The top of each row of benches was adorned with white ribbons, and some other good-smelling white flowers sat in huge vases on either side of the altar stairs.

He found himself unable to stand still, fidgeting and rocking back on his heels.

He'd never been so nervous in his life. At least Chantal sat in the front row, a familiar face to stare at. His mother had been disappointed that the wedding was taking place too quickly for her to attend, but said she understood. She made him promise to have Chantal take pictures, and sure enough, his sister had her camera in her lap, periodically blinding him with the flash.

His mother had then left explicit instructions that he was to bring Katya to Boston as soon as possible so they could have a reception there. That conversation had gone much easier than he'd thought.

One battle down, one to go. Only this one wasn't a battle. It was a forever-life-changing event, and he didn't feel the slightest bit prepared to take on a wife and all the responsibilities associated with caring for another person.

Yet it was his duty, and as his brother and sister reminded him, his destiny. He'd do what he had to do. All the Devlins would.

An old woman sat at the ancient organ and began to play. A haunting strain of beautiful but unfamiliar music echoed through the tiny chapel. Soon thereafter Elena came forward, dressed in a black full skirt and a long, flowing white blouse.

But Conner wasn't looking at Elena. His gaze was trained on the archway, and he was holding his breath.

He let it out when he saw Katya at the entryway, resisting the urge to whistle appreciatively.

God, she was a gorgeous woman. He didn't know where the wedding dress came from, but it was a body-hugging white velvet that billowed out into a long train behind her. She looked the part of the princess today, carrying herself regally. As she walked down the aisle, her gaze focused only on him.

His heart pounded like crazy, all the blood rushing from his head. He sure as hell hoped he wouldn't faint. Noah would never let him live it down.

If he didn't know better, he could swear Katya was scared to death. The flowers she held trembled and she looked so damn pale.

Marrying him couldn't be that scary, could it?

175

Maybe she was overwhelmed with everything happening so fast, like he was. That had to be it.

But when she arrived at the altar, Conner felt the icy chill of her fingers. And it wasn't cold in the chapel. She managed a tremulous smile, but her body was shaking.

Great. Now he had to worry about *her* fainting.

The mayor as well as a priest were present to provide both the civil and religious ceremony. All of it passed in a blur as words were spoken in Romanian and translated by Elena. When it came time to exchange rings, he pulled the ruby and diamond-encrusted ring from his pocket and slipped it onto Katya's finger.

"This was my grandmother's and was passed down to me to be given to the woman I chose to marry." Thank God for overnight express delivery. As soon as his mother heard he was getting married, she'd sent the ring.

Katya looked up at him and smiled. Really smiled this time, her face finally showing some color. Moisture pooled in her eyes and she said, "Thank you, Conner. It is truly beautiful and I am honored."

The rest of the ceremony moved quickly. He gathered Katya in his arms and told her without words how he felt, kissing her passionately. Her skin warmed and he scented her body's desire. His prime goal was to be alone with her as quickly as possible.

But that wasn't meant to be. At least not for a while. Apparently, Romanian wedding celebrations were steeped in tradition and that meant that they spent the better part of the day and into the night celebrating with everyone in Braslieu. At least Katya had spent some time over the past week teaching him some rudimentary phrases in Romanian, and more people spoke English than he originally thought.

Throughout it all, Chantal took pictures. So many that he wanted to take the fucking camera and toss it out the nearest window. Unfortunately, she guarded the damn thing like a momma wolf guarding her pup, claiming she was doing it for Mom.

Whatever. He was likely to suffer permanent eye damage from the flash going off so many times. He was certain that Chantal derived some kind of perverse pleasure in torturing him.

Finally, he had a chance to dance with his bride. His bride. His wife. God, he still couldn't believe all that had happened. Gathering her in his arms, he pulled her close, letting out a contented sigh.

"I've waited way too long to get you in my arms."

Katya smiled up at him. "It's almost over. Did you know it is customary for the Carpathian lupines to consummate their marriage outside under a full moon?"

Hell, yeah. The moon was full tonight. "I'm always happy to bow to custom."

"Only one more event and then we can be alone."

He rolled his eyes. "Now what? Grape stomping? Tree chopping? Rope climbing?"

She laughed and shook her head. "No. It's symbolic among my people, as I'm sure it is with yours."

"By people, are you meaning Romanian or lupine?"

"Carpathian and lupine."

Lord, if he had to perform another stupid task that required him to show his suitability as a husband, he'd need a stiff drink. "What is it this time?"

"It is customary for the alpha male to prove that the he is willing to share all that he has with the pack, that his mate will belong to all of the pack, symbolically speaking, of course."

It damn well better be symbolically speaking. "Which means what, exactly?"

"It means that I must have sex with you and another man tonight. Another lupine male."

Whatever happiness he felt dissipated in an instant. "What?"

"You don't do this in your marriage rituals?"

"Uhh, no." And if he had any say about this marriage, it wouldn't happen here, either.

"It is done with every marriage, Conner. And it is only a one-time occurrence. Every alpha male who has been mated must follow our customs."

His wedding night and he had to share his woman with some stranger? "I don't think so, Katya. I don't share what's mine."

She frowned. "I don't understand. You know I do not seek another mate. But I will follow lupine custom."

Fuck. "Well, it sure as hell would have been nice if you told me about this beforehand."

"I tried to yesterday. You kept brushing me off."

He remembered that now. She'd tried to tell him about the rituals and customs. "You could have forced me to listen. Didn't you realize how important this is?"

She shrugged. "I assumed you already knew, that your pack did the same thing. How was I to know it was unique to the Carpathians?"

"It's a big damn deal, Katya."

"Not to me. I suppose because it's simply another ritual, and not important to me as it obviously is to you."

"Fucking another guy is no big deal to you."

She studied him and pursed her lips, then smiled. "You're jealous."

A growl rumbled through his chest. "You're goddamn right I'm jealous. No man touches my woman. Ever."

She grinned. "I like that. Your woman." When she traced his cheek and jaw with the palm of her hand, his breathing quickened. He'd had enough of ceremony. He wanted his wife to himself now. He wanted to take her upstairs, peel off that sexy dress that hugged her curves, and lick every inch of her until he drove them both crazy.

When he imagined his wedding night, that's what he thought of. Not watching as his wife fucked another guy.

The music had stopped and they stood together in the center of the room.

"Conner, people are staring."

"I don't care. We need to talk about this, Katya."

"Very well." She took his hand and excused them as they walked through the crowd toward the kitchen. Dismissing the people cleaning up in there, she leaned against the counter. "Now, tell me what's wrong."

"What's wrong? What the hell do you think is wrong? Do you think I'm happy about having to share you with another man? Do I even get to be there to watch, or am I supposed to wait outside while you're happily fucked by some guy?"

She blushed and tugged her bottom lip between her teeth. "Actually, Conner, there are several witnesses."

This was getting better and better. "How many?"

"Everyone who wishes to attend as witness."

Christ! What the hell kind of civilization were they running up here? "I don't believe this."

She reached for his hand and pulled him toward her, wrapping her arms around his waist and laying her head against his chest. "I'm sorry. I thought you knew, that it was the same marriage rite practiced in your land. Here it is an ancient ritual, but one that has been passed down to every mated alpha since the beginning."

"I should have kidnapped you and taken you to Boston to get married."

She tilted her head back and smiled. "It would not have mattered. The ritual would still have taken place upon our return."

Dragging his hand through his hair, he pulled away and paced the kitchen. "I don't like this, Katya."

"I know. And it makes me happy that you don't want to share me."

He stopped and looked at her. "Be very clear on this. I will *never* share you. What's mine is mine. And you are most definitely *mine*."

The warmth in her eyes and the sexy way her lips curled when she smiled tore him apart. "And you are mine. If the situation were reversed and I was required to share you, I would not be happy about it, either. But I respect the customs of my people. As alpha, you will have to do the same."

He already knew that. But goddamn he hated this! "How does this work? Is some guy chosen at random, or has this been preordained?"

Hell, he didn't even have a beta yet. A beta would assist with these customs. He had a hell of a lot to learn here. There was so much pack business to take care of, and not nearly enough time to do it.

"Normally it would be the pack beta, but there isn't one."

"So who will it be, then?"

"Your beta. Your choice. It can be a substitute, any man of your choosing."

"I have to pick the guy?"

"Yes."

"It can be anyone I choose?"

"Of course."

He thought about it, but really, what choice did he have? There was only one person here that he trusted enough to take this impersonally. One person who could do it and walk away, and Conner would know he'd never infringe on his relationship with Katya.

"Noah. I choose Noah."

Katya's eyes widened, then she nodded. "I will go upstairs and prepare myself and will meet you in the clearing just inside the woods in an hour."

As she walked away, her hips swiveling in that soft, easy way that made him insane, his groin tightened and he hardened, wondering what it was going to be like to share her with his brother.

Other packs shared their females. It wasn't anything new. Hell, he'd participated in quite a few three-ways before. Never gave it a second thought.

The difference was he hadn't been in love with the women he'd fucked before. And that made his nerve endings feel raw and exposed, like someone poured acid on his skin. The thought of sharing Katya with anyone was like a punch to his gut.

But she was right. If he was going to be the alpha of the pack, then he had to adapt to their customs, not force his on them. And that meant he had to follow through with this, like it or not.

He spied Noah as he walked out of the kitchen and motioned to his brother, bringing him into the office and shutting the door.

"What's up?" Noah asked, leaning against the desk.

"We have a slight...problem."

Noah arched a brow. "What kind of problem?"

"There's a Carpathian lupine marriage ritual that I hadn't counted on. And it has to happen tonight."

"What is it? You don't have to sacrifice a chicken or anything, do you?"

"I wish it was that easy."

"Oh shit. Tell me."

"Katya has to fuck another man tonight."

Noah's eyes nearly fell out of his head.

Conner nodded. "Yeah, you heard right."

"Holy Christ, Con. Why?"

"It's their custom. The alpha male shares his female on the night of their marriage."

"Just tell her no. Refuse to do it."

He leaned against the table across from Noah and crossed his arms. "I wish it were that easy. But as Katya pointed out, and she's right, if I'm taking over as alpha, then I need to follow their customs and rituals."

"Okay. So who's the guy? And will he survive the night without you killing him?"

Conner laughed. "I hope so. Because I chose you."

Noah's eyes widened. "Me? No way. No thanks. I don't want any part of it."

"You'd rather have me watch her get fucked by a stranger, some guy that I'll have to worry about and maybe even have to kill if he ever looks at Katya again? Hell, Noah. You're the only one I trust to do this."

"Shit." Noah stood and walked to the window, staring out at the full moon. "You know I'd do anything for you, Con. But I don't want your woman."

"I know that. Which makes you perfect for this. I know you have no attachment to Katya. You'll be fulfilling an obligation."

Noah blew out a breath and dragged his hand through his hair. "It's one hell of an obligation."

"If you say no, I'll have to choose someone else. I hate this, Noah. And I know you do, too."

"How does Katya feel about it?"

"She's fine with it. Says it's a one-time thing, means nothing. I guess she's used to it since she's familiar with the customs here. It's not like a bomb was dropped on *her* tonight."

Noah turned around and faced him, a smirk lifting the corners of his mouth. "You're just worried she'll enjoy it too much."

"With you as my choice, I doubt it."

Noah laughed and shook his head. "I can't believe the shit I do for you, Con. So what's the game plan?"

# Chapter Thirteen

## ෩

Noah stood in the clearing with Conner, Elena and about a dozen other witnesses. Much fewer people than he expected. Then again, he supposed this wasn't a big deal to those who'd seen it before.

For that matter, it wasn't a big deal for him either. He wasn't a newcomer to the arena of ménages, and had shared women with other men before. He'd even had several women at once, and they'd shared each other.

Hell, he liked sex. Liked it a lot. And Katya had a fiery passion that he couldn't wait to taste.

But he didn't love her, and Conner did. And this ritual *was* a big damn deal to his brother. This wasn't just a woman to fuck and discard as if she meant nothing. Katya was his sister-in-law now. She was a Devlin. And he'd have to tread carefully in this event.

Shit. He really needed to finish up this task with Conner and get the hell off this mountain. Some solitude was definitely in order. Maybe one of the islands, or even the jungle. The sooner he got a new assignment from the agency, the better.

There was too much emotion here. This love crap was fine for other people, but not for him. God help him when it came his time to take on a pack and a mate. He sure as hell wasn't ready for it right now. He might never be.

As a wolf, he was wild, untamed and as free as the night air swirling above them. The human part of him craved the same freedom.

No, he'd be unlikely to settle down anytime soon, much to his mother's disappointment. Then again, she knew him better than anyone, knew he hated to be tied down. That's why he chose the career path he had. It allowed him freedom of movement and never required him to settle in one place too long.

He'd already been here too long and felt the burning itch to run.

But not yet. First, he had a task to fulfill. A last duty to his brother.

Making love to a beautiful woman wasn't exactly an arduous task. He'd never tell Conner, but he actually looked forward to it.

He glanced over at Elena, enjoying the way she devoured him with her hot eyes. If he read Elena's signals right, Katya wouldn't be the only woman he had tonight.

His cock rose and pressed against his pants, a fact that wasn't lost on the icy blonde. She was perfect for him. Wild and free, loving sex for the pure satisfaction and thrill of it. No strings required. Elena was no more ready for love and relationships than he was, which made her the ideal sex partner for him while he was here.

Soon enough, he'd leave her, too. Only she wouldn't care. And neither would he.

If only life could always be that simple.

* * * * *

Katya headed into the woods, trying to summon up the courage to get through what came next. She wanted to be locked in her bedroom with her husband and spend the remainder of the night making hot, fiery love with him. But she had an obligation to fulfill first. Once that was done, she could start on her new life with Conner.

What was going to happen tonight made her nervous. First, because she never wanted anyone other than Conner to touch her. And two, because she worried he would think she desired another man.

Granted, if she had to choose another to partake in the ritual, she couldn't ask for one better than Noah. Not only was he ruggedly handsome, but he walked and talked with an inherent eroticism that intrigued her. The man had to be good, and despite the fact she was wholly and completely in love with Conner, the idea of having Noah just once wasn't at all unpleasant.

The bond Noah and Conner shared was evident. That made what was going to happen easier than if Conner was forced to share her with a stranger. Besides, she didn't think she could tolerate another man's touch. Noah, on the other hand, was family now. And that she could deal with. He and Conner were so close in looks and temperament that it would be like making love to a mirror image of her husband.

Her nipples hardened against the thin gown, her pussy clenching in anticipation of what would occur.

People had already assembled in the clearing. Not everyone who lived in and around the castle would attend, but they only required an audience for the first portion of the event. She saw Conner and Noah talking to Elena, who was no doubt explaining the steps of the ritual to them. Conner turned before she'd even cleared the last copse of trees. His eyes met hers and they connected on a level reserved only for the two of them.

He smiled, and she knew everything would be all right. Noah turned next and grinned, arching a brow. His gaze roamed appreciatively over her body and she felt her cunt moisten.

Conner met her halfway and wrapped his arms around her, kissing her neck. She shivered at the heated touch of his mouth to her skin. When he pulled back, he looked her directly in the eyes.

"Since you've never had another man but me, this is an opportunity for you to experience what it's like. After this, I won't have to worry that you'll spend the rest of your life wondering what it would have been like to fuck another man."

His generosity surprised her, and thrilled her at the same time. Knowing he was accepting of the ritual made what she was required to do so much easier. She reached for his face, touching his lips with her fingertips. "I won't ever need another man. You are all I want."

She may not be able to declare her love for him, but she could at least tell him that she wanted no one else but him. Right now, it was the most her heart would allow.

His eyes blazed hot, turning molten golden green. "And you are all I want. Shall we get this over with so we can spend the rest of our wedding night alone?"

The teasing glint in his gaze relaxed her completely. She slipped her hand into his and allowed him to lead her to the center of the clearing.

Noah approached and took her other hand. The warmth and strength of having two men by her side was comforting. Noah nodded and sent her a reassuring smile, then bent and kissed her cheek, whispering, "I'm much better at sex than Conner, but try to restrain your desire to leave him for me."

She giggled, knowing he teased her. When she looked to Conner, he just rolled his eyes.

Elena stepped forward and began to recite the ritual in Romanian. Katya translated for Conner and Noah.

"It is the custom of our people to share the mate of the alpha male with another male. This occurs on the night of the marriage of an alpha to his life mate. In this we ensure that the alpha acknowledges he belongs to the pack, his mate belongs to the pack, and the pack belongs to him. You will begin by disrobing each other. The act of possession can take place in any way the parties wish. Conner makes the choice. It can be oral, anal or vaginal penetration, or all three. Once it is over and fulfillment is reached, the ritual ends. What happens afterward is up to the participants, but no further witnesses are required."

"It all sounds so clinical," Conner whispered.

"Yeah, but fun," Noah said.

Katya smiled at the differences in opinion between the two brothers. Of course, to Noah this was just a one-time opportunity for sex. For Conner, it went deeper. And she loved him for that.

After she finished her speech, Elena turned back to them. Her heated gaze raked over Noah, centering on his crotch while she licked her lips hungrily. Katya got the idea that Noah would be entertained elsewhere when he finished the ritual this evening.

"Shall we begin?" Katya asked, anxious to get this over with as quickly as possible so she could begin her life with Conner.

"You're in charge here, baby," Conner said. "Go ahead and start. We'll take this at your pace."

She looked up at the moon, its silver beauty and power compelling her, bringing out the primal beast in her and reminding her that animal passion was part of her nature. She turned to Conner. "Kiss me."

His gaze gleamed hot and he pulled her against his hard chest. His lips touched hers gently at first, then with hard, passionate possession. She drank in his fiery kiss and gave the same back to him, lost in the sensations of being held in his arms.

Oh, what she wouldn't give to share this moment alone with him! And she knew he wanted it that way, too.

But then Noah stepped behind her, the heat of his body tripping along her nerve endings. She inhaled, taking in the scent of him. He was aroused, primed and ready so quickly. He ran his hands over her shoulders and down his arms. His cock nestled against her buttocks as his mouth came down on her neck, singeing her skin.

She shuddered and looked at Conner, his lips curling upward. "I'll bet every woman wants to know what it's like to be taken by two men." He cupped her chin and traced her jawline with one fingertip. "Did you ever wonder what that felt like, Katya?"

"Yes," she said, shuddering at Noah's tongue raking her neck. "In my fantasies I sometimes imagined two men making love to me."

"Your fantasy is about to become a reality, baby. Are you ready for this?"

Surprisingly, she was. What had started as ritual and required now became an intense desire to experience lovemaking with two men. To be the center of attention between two alpha males was more than she could have ever imagined. She couldn't have chosen a better third for this ritual than Noah. His powerful body rocked against her back and buttocks. He reached around her to unbutton her gown and slide it off her shoulders.

When it pooled at her feet, Conner's gaze grew hot. "You are so beautiful." He circled her nipples with the tips of his fingers, smiling when the buds puckered and stood erect.

Noah cupped her breasts, holding them out for Conner. He bent over to lick one, then the other. She leaned back against Noah, her senses filled with the overwhelming sensation of two men touching her.

"Undress," she managed, needing to feel naked skin against her.

She heard the rustle of clothing behind her while her gaze was glued to Conner as he quickly shed his clothes. She admired his flat abdomen, then looked lower, following the line of dark hair as it ended in a nest above his cock.

She couldn't resist the smile and smug sense of satisfaction. That beautiful body belonged to her, now. She could have it anytime she wanted it.

"Keep looking at me like that and Noah isn't even going to get a chance. I'll be inside you before he has a chance to get hard."

"Wanna bet?" Noah said.

Before she could respond to Conner's tease, Noah had turned her around to face him.

Conner's brother wasn't unpleasant to look at, either. Though not as tall as Conner, he was broader in the shoulders and thighs. Powerful muscles spanned his massive chest. Where Conner was well-muscled and possessed the body of a runner, Noah's body spoke of power and strength.

She arched a brow and studied the curling mat of hair on his chest, then followed that dark trail to a very long, very thick cock.

"Like what you see?" he asked.

When she looked up and met the teasing glint in his amber eyes, she nodded. "Very much."

Conner pressed against her back, sweeping her hair to the side and nibbling the side of her neck.

Noah brushed his lips against hers. He tasted like sex, his scent filled with the barely leashed power she sensed he held in check.

Unbridled, Noah would be formidable, indeed.

"I'll take very good care of you tonight, princess," Noah murmured against her lips, then turned her around to face Conner once again.

Her husband took her mouth in a fiery kiss, as if he wanted to erase the touch of Noah's lips against hers. She met his passion eagerly, sliding her tongue inside his mouth.

Noah kissed her neck, his lips blazing a heated trail down her spine. The leaves underneath them crunched as Noah's hot tongue swirled over first one buttock, then the other. Then he dipped to his knees, nudging her legs apart.

Delicious sensations licked over her heated skin as Conner crouched, too. He nuzzled her sex, his tongue snaking out to taste her. She bit her lower lip and caressed his dark hair, knowing it wouldn't take long to reach an orgasm. Especially when Noah parted the flesh of her buttocks and probed her anus with his tongue.

She whimpered, her gaze focused on Conner, but feeling the wicked touch of another man's tongue behind her was indescribable. She wished she could watch both men pleasure her.

Noah's fingers dug into her hips, squeezing as his tongue slid into her tight hole. At the same time, Conner tongue-fucked her pussy like a tiny cock, drinking in the juices that poured from her slit.

"Please," she begged, not even knowing what she asked for. The dual pleasures were too much too bear and she was helpless against the sensations bombarding her. When Conner covered her clit and sucked, she catapulted over the edge with a loud cry of fulfillment, her cream flooding his hot tongue. Relentless, he refused to stop despite her nails digging into his shoulders. Noah continued to plunge his tongue inside her puckered hole, driving her into another orgasm more powerful than the first.

Her legs trembled and she could barely stand. Conner lay back on the ground and pulled her on top of him, dragging her mouth down to his.

She tasted her completion on his lips and licked her own juices, cleaning his mouth and chin like a kitten lapping up sweet milk. He groaned, his cock jutting between her thighs. She rocked her pussy against its length, rewarded with his deep groan.

What wondrous magic this was! She had no idea that having two men pleasure her could be this fulfilling. And yet despite the passion she encountered with both Conner and Noah, she knew her heart belonged only to one.

Her alpha. Her husband. The man she loved. Yet she still couldn't find the words to tell him how she felt. Words that, once spoken, made her vulnerable to loss again.

She never wanted to feel that way again. Forcing the clenching pain away, she devoured Conner's mouth, sliding her soaked pussy against his blazing hot cock.

His breath was ragged as he pulled his mouth away and spoke. "Fuck me, Katya."

Spasms squeezed her womb at his erotic words. She turned and noticed the others watching. Some had disrobed and had begun to fuck the nearest partner. Others, like Elena, touched themselves through their clothing. She'd been so caught up in the whirlwind of sensations created by Conner and Noah that she'd completely forgotten they had an audience.

For her, there were only two men in existence right now. And she found herself wanting much, much more of the sweet pleasure.

Conner inhaled sharply as Katya raked her sweet cunt over his hard flesh. As much as he loved the times they'd made love before, there was something very special about this time. Maybe it was the full moon, which always increased his reactions to anything primal or sensual. Maybe it was the fact that his new bride responded to both him and Noah with such wild abandon. And maybe he was just in love with her, and that made sex that much more special.

Hell, he didn't know, and right now, he didn't care. He'd even tuned out the witnesses until just now, then realized they were all seeking their own pleasure. Elena's dark gaze focused on Noah as she rubbed her nipples with one hand, the other stuffed inside her pants, busily stroking her pussy. His cock lurched against Katya's moist slit, and more juices poured onto his balls.

Noah loomed above them, mostly silent, his expression intent as he stroked and kissed Katya's back and buttocks.

It was time to get past this point and move on.

"Come on, baby. Slide that hot pussy over my dick and fuck me," he urged, then nodded to his brother.

Noah stood and moved over to Katya's side. Fuck, his cock was hard. He needed release after tasting the fiery beauty. When she came, her scent poured over him, her sweet cream dripping between her legs and he couldn't resist a taste of her pussy juice.

Katya was one amazingly passionate woman. And his brother didn't deserve to be so fucking lucky. As he stood there watching Katya lower herself onto Conner's shaft, her head tilted back and a look of such emotion on her face, a pang that Noah had never felt before hit him in the gut.

What the hell was it? Regret? Did he actually feel remorse that he was missing out on a relationship like this?

No way. Noah didn't need women for anything other than fucking and as an occasional partner on a mission. Other than his family, he lived alone, did his work alone, and liked it just fine. When he needed a woman, one was always handy, no matter what part of the world he occupied at the time.

But just now, seeing the way Katya responded to Conner, he knew it was more than physical pleasure between the two of them. He actually felt the emotions swirling around them. Unfamiliar emotions. Deep emotions.

Like love.

He knew right then that he wasn't complete, that there was something lacking in his life.

Sonofabitch! He didn't want to have these kinds of feelings. Not now, not ever.

Determined to avoid any further thought about relationships and women, he palmed his cock and stroked it, stepping toward Katya. She turned to him and smiled, and when she licked her lips in anticipation he nearly lost it.

Oh yeah. He wanted that mouth on his cock.

He reached for the back of her head and drew her closer to the throbbing tip of his shaft. Drops of pre-cum teetered on the edge, and her tongue snaked out to capture the fluid before it fell to the forest floor.

"God, baby, what a sweet mouth you have. Suck it, Katya."

Her lips covered him and he closed his eyes, determined to block out anything and everything but the erotic pleasure he received from Katya's mouth.

Katya licked the head of Noah's cock, taking the thick shaft in deeply, then moving back to watch her saliva cover the mushroomed head. She looked up and watched him. Lord, the man was magnificent standing there with one hand wrapped around the back of her head, the other massaging his balls as she sucked his magnificent rod.

His tangy taste and the velvet smoothness of the head of his cock made her pussy clench around Conner's shaft. She rocked forward and back, her clit hitting the base of his cock and splintering sparks of need deep inside her.

In response to her movements, Conner lifted his hips, thrusting harder and faster inside her aching cunt until she thought she'd die from the pleasure.

She moved Noah's hand away and cupped the twin sacs underneath his shaft, squeezing and tugging them gently. He groaned and pushed her head closer, forcing more of his delicious cock into her mouth. Deeper, harder, until she swallowed his cock head.

For an alpha female, this was supreme delight. To have both these powerful men under her control was more satisfying than she realized. She was in charge of their pleasure, she directed each sensation with either her mouth or her pussy.

And she loved it.

Even better, they loved it.

The scent of their arousal filled the air around her. Conner reached for her breasts, plucking her erect nipples and sending spiraling sensation to her cunt. She could do nothing but groan against Noah's cock, which caused him to pump faster and harder against her mouth.

Pleasure built, higher and higher like a coiling snake threatening to strike.

"Come for me, baby," Conner urged, his voice a hot whisper in the night. "Let me feel that pussy squeeze the juice right out of me."

Conner helped that suggestion by reaching between her legs and stroking her clit with his thumb. Fire burst within her and she whimpered, sucking harder at Noah's cock.

"Aww, Christ, Katya," Noah responded, wrapping his fist in her hair and pumping hard, jettisoning a hot spurt of fluid into her throat. She swallowed greedily as the sensations in her lower belly spread out like a wildfire.

Noah withdrew and she turned her attention to Conner, lifting her hips and slamming them down over his shaft. He thrummed her clit faster and faster, the sensations tightening inside her. When he groaned and dug his fingers into her hips, she erupted, her orgasm shooting fiery lightning in front of her eyes and pouring out her creamy cum all over Conner's cock and balls.

She came, and then came again, her gaze focused on Conner. The way his eyes lit up with the feral light of the animal within him, his claws unsheathing to scrape her skin, his teeth and jaw elongating as his orgasm forced the change within him.

And the animal in her surfaced as she continued to ride out her climax, growling and dropping her head to his chest to take a sharp bite of his sweet flesh. Time suspended and she was lost in the spiraling emotions of completion, more satisfied than she'd ever been before.

This was perfection and she never wanted the moment to end.

She couldn't move. Conner's heart raced against her cheek. He wrapped his arms around her, seemingly in no hurry to move from their spot on the forest floor. Barely able to open her eyes, she lifted her lids partway to survey the area around them.

Everyone else had gone.

The ritual was over.

Conner and Noah had given her a magic that she never knew, had never thought possible.

But now that it was finished, she only wanted to wrap her body around her husband and never let him go.

The conflicts within her surfaced as she opened her mouth to let the words of her heart spill free. But still, that familiar hesitancy reared its head—that need to keep her protective wall up so that she couldn't be hurt again.

Conner kissed the top of her head. "You ready to go inside now?"

She leaned up and searched his face. "Let's shift and run."

His gaze gleamed dark. "You just want to fuck me as a wolf."

"Well, yes, that, too."

She climbed off and he stood, reaching out his hand to her.

"Come on, wild woman. Let's see if your wolf ass is as hot looking as the human one."

She shifted and took off at a run, knowing the game of chase they played up the mountain would end with passionate lovemaking under the full moon.

Her newly married life was starting out very, very well. And if she couldn't let herself feel the love that she knew she had for Conner, then this would just have to be good enough.

# Chapter Fourteen

ഔ

Conner inhaled the sharp pine scent of the forest around them. Lying naked with Katya in his arms, they didn't feel the cold at such a high elevation despite the early morning chill.

Not even dawn yet, the moon still hung over the horizon, calling to him.

Not a chance this time. He was exhausted. With the wedding yesterday and then the ritual followed by the run in the woods with Katya, they'd had a damn full day. He and Katya had run up the mountain, stopping when they reached a small cliff near the top.

There, they'd made love in wolf form, both of them howling into the night for what seemed like hours. When they were spent, they made the climb to the top of the mountain and fell asleep.

Katya turned and nestled against his side, one leg thrown over his hips. Her thigh brushed his cock and it twitched to life again.

He shook his head. Damn thing was out of control. His body was exhausted. His cock thought it was some kind of superhero.

*Down boy. I'm too damn tired.*

The low howls of a wolf pack echoed through the forest below.

His pack. His family now. Curling an arm possessively around Katya, he leaned in and breathed the sweet scent of her hair.

He hadn't even told her he loved her yet, but he'd rectify that as soon as she woke. Now he was content to have her in his arms and listen to the sounds of—

Gunfire! The echo of gunshots was followed by the howls of the wolf pack. He didn't have to wake Katya. She bolted upright, her eyes widening.

"Hunters!" she cried, scurrying to her feet and taking off down the mountain.

He didn't bother to argue with her, just caught up to her and ran like hell.

Both of them shifted along the way, Conner taking the lead as they leapt over limbs, rocks and various roots, more sure-footed as wolves and ten times faster than if they were in human form.

His senses keen in this form, he inhaled, scenting the area around them.

Would he be able to communicate with Katya this way? The psychic connection didn't always work.

*Several different human scents*, he thought.

*Yes. I know very well the smell of the hunters.*

He nodded, pleased that he and Katya were able to communicate so well in this form. He wondered where Noah was, and if he was with the pack or inside the castle. He could sure use his brother's tracking skills right now.

*Tread light. I don't want them spotting us until we can get a feel for how many and where.*

She lifted her snout and nodded, staying right behind his left hindquarter.

Perfect.

They entered the flatlands of the forest and crept along slowly, following the sounds and scents of both the packs and the hunters.

*Sounds like about twenty hunters*, Katya communicated. *That's a big hunt.*

So much for the cooperation of the ministry. Conner wondered if the man had been blowing smoke up his ass with promises of protection, all the while knowing that some obscure head count of wolves would lead to the hunters' right to take down a certain number.

Well, that "certain number" was his pack now, and by God they weren't going to be allowed to just cull the pack whenever they thought the numbers were too big.

*Let me go around the left and you take the right*, Katya suggested.

*No. I want you with me.*

*I can protect you better if I can come at them from behind.*

He didn't care. He didn't want to take any chances on Katya being injured. If she stood next to him the entire time, he could get in between her and a hunter's bullet. If she circled around to the other side, she could be ambushed or hit straight on. No way was he going to lose her.

*I don't need you to protect me, Conner. I've done this before. I can take care of myself. We're much smarter than they are, you know.*

*I know that. Just stay here, Katya.*

*But —*

He growled a warning to her and she snarled back, but took her place at his flank. Satisfied that she was where he could keep an eye on her, he circled the outskirts of the hunters' positions, counting them one by one.

There were about a dozen of them, stalking his pack as if they were nothing but a pelt or a trophy. They disgusted him. Didn't they realize that the wolves were endangered, regardless of the bogus numbers they put up about the surplus of wolves in the Carpathians? Not that the hunters cared. They weren't managing the numbers. They were hunting for the thrill of the kill.

Not this time. Not anymore. He wasn't going to give the ministry any reason to want to launch a hunt of the wolves, so no way would he injure them.

But he could sure scare the shit out of them.

As two of the hunters stalked a young wolf trying to hide, he stepped calmly behind them, then let out a howl that would curl any human's hair.

The hunters screamed like little girls, turned around and ran like their asses were on fire.

Katya growled appreciatively. *I hope they pissed their pants.*

He smiled, baring his teeth, lusting to take a bite out of those asses. But he'd have to content himself with merely moving them away from the pack.

They did the same thing with another pair of hunters, sneaking up behind them and then growling and scaring them away.

That part was fun.

The other wolves had spread out, forcing the hunters to split up in pairs.

*I told we've handled this before,* Katya informed him.

*Your people do well. We should be able to –*

He stilled when he scented lupine on the air first, but not full wolf. One of the pack in human form? That couldn't be. But when he turned, he realized why.

Peter, in hunting gear, stalking the wolves.

Katya spotted him too, her growl low but loud enough for Peter's keen lupine senses to hear. He spun around, his face twisted in a sick smile, and took aim at Katya. Conner's reaction was swift as he leapt in the air and came down on top of Peter. Peter dropped the gun and fought, screaming as Conner bit into his shoulder.

Peter shifted, his strength increasing as he made a rapid change to wolf. But Conner's rage was stronger than Peter's desperate attempts and he quickly had him pinned, his teeth clamping down on Peter's throat. The smell of fear filled the air around them. Conner growled, his canines digging into the fur of his adversary's neck.

But Peter went still, lying limp. And just as suddenly, shifted back to human.

"Got you just where I want you," he choked, his eyes feral, his sanity gone.

Conner heard Katya's raging snarl just as the sound of rifle shot reverberated through the forest. A fiery hot pain seared Conner's chest, followed by a numbing warmth.

Shit. That shot had hit him.

Thank God it hadn't hit Katya. He heard her in his mind, felt her presence as she drew closer. He heard a hunter's scream and knew Katya had attacked.

Conner felt the dizziness, the weakness, but managed to hold on long enough to look down at Peter, whose eyes widened.

*Yes, you sonofabitch. You shouldn't have shifted back to human so quickly.* Peter began the swift transformation to wolf, but not swift enough. Conner bit down hard, ending Peter's life. He felt no remorse for killing a lupine. This wolf was a traitor to the pack and deserved to die.

He let loose of Peter's lifeless body and stumbled, barely able to keep on all fours. Wetness seeped down his chest and he fell again, this time unable to get back up.

He searched the forest for Katya but didn't see her. He'd die if she wasn't all right. He still hadn't told her he loved her. Dammit, it was important that she knew how he felt.

Later. There'd be time to tell her later, right? Now he was tired. His world shifted and went black.

* * * * *

"Hurry. Get him upstairs," she ordered, thankful that even unconscious, Conner's body had known to shift back to his human form. Treating him would be much easier without having to search through thick fur for injuries.

Noah met her at the foot of the stairs. "What happened?"

"It was Peter. He brought the hunters in. Conner and Peter were fighting and Peter shifted back to human. One of the hunters shot Conner, thinking a wolf attacked a human."

Noah nodded and reached for his brother, carrying him effortlessly up the staircase. She read the panic on his face, the same panic she knew was reflected in her own.

Chantal met them at the top of the stairs, blinking back sleep. Her eyes widened as she spotted her brother. "Oh, God," she whispered, her eyes filling with tears. "He's been shot?"

"Yes," Katya answered, taking Chantal's hand as they headed to the bedroom.

Guilt stabbed at her. How could she have been so careless as to let this happen? Why did Conner step between her and Peter? If he hadn't, she'd have easily skirted the bullet and hidden, or attacked Peter herself. She knew she would have sensed him before it was too late.

"Lay him on the bed," she directed Noah, jerking the coverlet back while Noah set his brother onto the mattress.

Having a lupine doctor on hand was a blessing, since the nearest hospital was in Bucharest. Besides, they could not explain a gunshot wound to the hospital staff there and the trip would take the better part of a day. Conner could be dead by then.

The pack physician, Mikail, followed them to the bedroom and immediately set to work checking Conner's injuries. Katya stood at the side of the bed, trying not to panic at the sight of so much blood pouring from the wound on Conner's chest. The doctor worked on him for what seemed like hours. She paced, but all she really wanted to do was curl up in a ball on the bed next to him and hope she wasn't going to lose someone else that she loved.

No. She refused to think of either losing him or of loving him.

*Love is a fantasy. He is a good partner. A strong alpha. If he dies, you will find another.*

It was the mantra she had repeated to herself over and over since the moment she realized her emotions for Conner ran much deeper than she wanted them to. Staying remote made losing him easier. If only she could convince herself to be that heartless.

She glanced down at him. So pale, his lips nearly blue, his chest rising and falling with supreme effort. Her sense of hearing picked up the bubbling rattle of his breathing, as if he was drowning in the thick, flowing blood filling his lungs.

Her gaze flitted over to Noah. He frowned, looked almost angry. Deep lines etched his forehead and she knew he was as concerned as she was. But he hadn't said a word. Just stared down at Conner, looking more like he wanted to strangle his brother.

Chantal held tight to her hands as if she was her only lifeline. Katya squeezed back, not knowing what to say to offer comfort.

Mikail stood and turned to her. "The bullet just missed his heart. In that respect, he was very lucky. However, he's lost a lot of blood, and his left lung has collapsed. He needs a chest tube. Katya, he needs more than what I can do for him."

The bleak look on Mikail's face told her more than she needed to know.

"He's going to die, isn't he?"

"I don't know."

Noah cursed and turned on his heel, his fists balled up at his side. He left without a word. Chantal let out an anguished sob and rushed out of the room after him.

She felt their anguish, but could do nothing to help them. Her heart fisted in pain, so unbearable she nearly dropped to her knees. How could this have happened? She couldn't have found him only to lose him so quickly.

*Not again. Please, God, don't do this to me again.*

"He is lupine, Katya," Mikail said. "You know we recuperate much faster than humans."

Suddenly shivering, she wrapped her arms around her middle and shook her head. "You said he needs more care. More than what his healing powers are capable of."

Mikail stood. "All we can do is watch him for the next twenty-four hours, see if his body is strong enough to repair itself. Sometimes the damage is too great, as you know."

Yes, she knew. She'd watched her parents die, knowing there was nothing she could do to save them.

Mikail left, promising to come in every hour and check on Conner. He left instructions for two of his assistants to take turns watching over him and to alert him if there were any changes.

But she couldn't just sit here and wait for him to die, watch his breathing slow more and more each hour until he just…stopped.

No! She wouldn't go through it again! Never again. Pushing past the woman who'd entered the room to sit with Conner, she hurried down the stairs, ignoring the concerned looks from the people lining the staircase and standing below.

She couldn't speak to them, couldn't tell them that their new alpha had sacrificed his life to save hers. She brushed past them and hurried through the door, running toward the woods at the end of the path. Inhaling the pine scent, she began to strip as soon as she stepped into the forest, then shifted, running nonstop with no direction in mind.

While she ran for her mountains, she practiced hardening her heart against losing Conner. Actually, she barely knew him. It would be easy to get over the loss. It wasn't the same as her parents. She didn't rely on him, he hadn't been around that long.

She hadn't even told him she loved him.

Finally out of breath, she tipped her snout up and howled at the morning sun coming up over the horizon. The changing from night to day, season to season, year to year.

Life went on. But Conner wouldn't.

And she'd get over it. Strength had always been her salvation. It had seen her through the death of her parents, it would see her through the death of her husband.

The wolves of the Carpathians surrounded her, one by one moving slowly toward her, their heads bowed, their pain evident.

They knew what had happened, and they cared. They hurt. Despite the fact they didn't even know Conner, his pain was their pain.

They felt. Something she had tried to deny, but could no longer hide from.

Loving someone meant taking the risk of losing them. She had to face the pain, to feel the love she'd tried so hard to deny.

The humanity within her took control and she shifted, falling to her knees and sobbing for what she was going to lose. The wolves stayed close, lying down beside her and watching her with mournful eyes.

"I love him," she whispered to them. "I love him and I don't want to lose him."

They didn't respond, but she felt them within her, giving her the strength she needed to face what was to come. Her time of cowardice was over. It was time to go back and hold her husband's hand, to will him to recover, or stand by his side until the end.

The sun had climbed nearly overhead by the time she made it back to the castle, dressing quickly and hurrying up the stairs. Inhaling deeply, she was determined to face whatever happened in there.

Noah and Chantal were in there with Conner, their faces as grim as they had been when she'd seen them last. Her gaze flitted to her husband, and she fought back tears as she saw how deathly pale he had become.

"No change?" she whispered to Chantal, sitting down beside Conner.

"No."

"Have you called your parents?"

"Yes, but I told them not to come. There's not enough time for them to get here. If he survives, they can come then. If he doesn't, there's no point."

She didn't question Noah's decision, just nodded.

"I had to leave," she started, feeling the need to explain to them why. "I was afraid of losing him. I didn't think I'd be able to face another loss of someone I loved."

Saying the words made her feel more the coward than ever. She dropped her chin to her chest, ashamed to look at them.

Chantal squeezed her hand. "We understand, honey. Besides, there's nothing any of us can do right now except wait. It's up to Conner now."

She nodded, but the remorse didn't lessen. Her place was by his side. Comforting him, encouraging him to heal. Instead, she had run away and hidden, afraid to face reality like an adult.

It was time to grow up.

"Conner, listen to me," she said, sitting down beside him to hold his hand. "You need to heal. Tell your body to heal. I need you."

The words spilled along with the tears, but this time she didn't run. "I love you, Conner Devlin. Don't you dare leave me now. We've gone through hell together in such a short period of time. That means we have a destiny, a purpose. I need you to survive, to use your strength to heal. Come back to me, love. We have babies to make, a dynasty to create."

She sat by his side until the sun had shifted into the western sky, slowly lowering and bringing on the night. The moon was still full, shining in through the windows of the bedroom, its silver glow reflecting off Conner's deathly white complexion.

Long after she had made the others leave, she sat there, talking to him. Sometimes cajoling and teasing, sometimes crying quietly, and other times railing at him, screaming at him to find the strength within him to fight it off.

She would not lose him!

Fearing he'd drift away from her if she wasn't there watching him every second, she kept her vigil, unable to eat, sleep or leave his side. Chantal finally came in and forced her to get up and stretch, promising if there was any change while she showered and got something to eat she'd let her know immediately.

Knowing that his sister had as much right to be by Conner's side as she did, she took her advice. After showering, she slipped into the kitchen and found Noah there, downing a glass of ale.

She nodded to him, then fixed herself a sandwich, automatically preparing one for him, too. They ate side by side at the table, never once saying a word to each other.

No words were necessary. They both knew what the other felt. When they finished eating, she washed the dishes and dried her hands on the towel. Noah was right behind her when she turned around.

She fell against his chest, sobbing. He wrapped his strong arms around her and held her, stroking her hair as she let out the pain tearing her apart inside. When she finished, she looked up at him and said, "I love him so much, Noah. I'll never survive if I lose him."

Was that moisture glistening in Noah's eyes? He set his chin firmly and said, "You won't lose him. He's strong. He's fighting this, Katya. That's why he's still with us. Go back up there, hold his hand, and tell him how you feel. He needs to hear it."

He kissed her forehead and she hurried back upstairs.

"Anything?" she asked Chantal.

"Nothing. I'm sorry. I need to go make some phone calls." Chantal stood, then hugged her tight. Katya drank in the support of his family, needing it more than she could ever tell them.

"Are you okay?" she asked Chantal.

She nodded. "I'll be fine. He'll be fine. I know he will."

"That's what Noah said."

"He's right. Believe it. We know our brother. He's too damn stubborn to die."

She managed an encouraging smile for Chantal, then turned to Conner as soon as Chantal left the room.

Still pale, but did it seem as if there was a little more color in his face than there had been this morning, or was she just imagining it?

When she sat next to him and slid her hand within his, it felt…warmer. Still a bit chilled, but definitely more heat than the near-deathly cold temperature of earlier.

Hope surged within her, and she leaned in, pressing her lips against his. Whispering in his ear, she said, "Conner, I love you. Please come back to me."

A groan came from his lips, and she could have shouted at the rafters. "Conner, can you hear me?"

As if sunlight streamed into the room despite the darkness of night, his skin began to color again, his normal healthy tan returning in minutes. He opened his eyes and frowned. "Did we oversleep?"

She laughed and cried at the same time, leaning over to kiss him. "It's a brand-new day, my love!" Hurrying to the door, she shouted for Noah and Chantal, who came running.

Too excited to stand still, she rocked on her heels when they rushed in and hugged him. Conner glared at Noah when Noah threw his arms around him.

"What the hell is going on?" he asked.

"You were shot, dumbass. Don't you remember?" Noah replied.

"Not a damn thing. Oh, wait, the hunters." He turned to Katya. "Peter. Sonofabitch. Peter brought the hunters in here. He tried to kill you. And I killed him, instead." He reached for his chest and felt the bandage, then looked back up at her. "I guess I didn't die."

Katya laughed and swiped away the tears, perching on the bed next to him. "No, thank God. You didn't die."

He swept her hair away from her neck. "You look beautiful. I love you, Katya. I don't want to miss the opportunity to say that, in case I drop dead in the next few minutes."

Her skin broke out in chills, the moment too incredible to comprehend. His touch sent her heart soaring, his smile touched her soul. She thought she'd never feel the warmth of his hands on her again. "I love you, too, Conner."

The tears wouldn't stop, but she didn't care.

She had the man she loved back. For the first time in her life, she started to think that there was actually something to look forward to.

# Chapter Fifteen

ॐ

"Would you all quit hovering over me like I'm going to expire in the next five minutes?"

"Now what would Mom say if she knew we'd let you get out of bed before you're ready?" Chantal asked with a smug smile.

"I've already talked to Mom and she knows I feel fine."

"You look pretty weak to me," Noah quipped.

"Barely able to stand on your own, actually," Chantal added.

"You're both full of shit. That's how I know I'm all better now. The two of you are annoying me."

"Ah, well, maybe things are back to normal again," Noah said. "Maybe it's time we both take our leave of Braslieu so we can get on with our own lives."

He should be so lucky. Conner glared at his brother and sister and swung his legs over the side of the bed, the sheet nestled in his crotch. Chantal glowered back, and Noah just grinned.

"I'm naked. I'm getting up. Get out."

For the past twenty-four hours they had been driving him nuts. Catering to him, not letting him get up except to go to the bathroom. He needed a shower, a shave, and he wanted a goddamn steak, not the flimsy excuses for food they'd been bringing him.

Soup. Who the fuck ate soup as a meal? His body was fine. His recuperative powers restored, he was more than ready to assume his normal responsibilities.

Though he really did enjoy the part where Katya spent every moment with him. They'd spent a lot of time talking, which was all she'd allow, since she told him he wasn't nearly well enough for what *he* had in mind.

Ha! That's what she thought. By the time he'd cleaned up, then had Noah sneak him in a huge steak dinner, he felt refreshed, strong, and horny as hell.

The next stop on his trip to full recovery was having his wife for dessert.

He'd missed her touch, her scent, the feel of her soft ass nestled in his crotch when they slept at night. He missed the perky tips of her breasts and the sweet honey of her pussy.

And he was going to take possession of all of those...tonight.

Slipping under the sheets, he leaned against the headboard and waited for her.

True to form, she breezed through the doorway. She hadn't left him for more than a couple hours at a time since he'd awakened from the long sleep that had healed his body.

"You look great," she said, her smile brightening the room more than any artificial light could.

"So do you." Edible, in fact.

"Are you tired? How do you feel?" She pressed her palm to his forehead. He took the opportunity to peek down her blouse, wishing he could lick between her breasts.

Soon. "Yeah, I'm kind of tired. Ready to go to bed?"

"Sure. Let me go take a shower and I'll be right back."

He waited, his cock getting harder by the minute as he thought of all the things he wanted to do with Katya. Listening to the sounds she made while she showered, the way she hummed when she combed her hair, the smell of the lotion she slathered all over her body, had his balls aching by the time she came out of the bathroom in all her naked glory.

Her damp hair fell in waves, sections of it partially hiding her nipples. The soft lips of her pussy were visible as she moved toward him. His cock lurched against the sheet and he put his hands in his lap to disguise the evidence of his need.

Did she have any idea how sexy she was when she walked? God, he was hungry.

Ravenous, in fact. Starving to death for a taste of his woman.

Naked, she slipped into bed and turned off the light, ready to curl up next to him…barely next to him…like she had last night.

But not this time. This time, he had a big surprise for her.

"Conner!" she squealed when he pulled her against him and nestled his hard cock between her buttocks. She scooted away, flipped on the light and looked down at his cock as if she never expected to see him with a hard-on again. "How did *that* happen?"

He grinned. "In the usual way. I've been thinking about you."

She kept glancing at his shaft. "Are you sure you're up to this?"

"What do you think?"

Finally, the concerned frown lines on her face diminished, and she smiled. "Good. I've been waiting for you to feel up to it again."

"Baby, I'm up."

She grinned. "Make love to me, Conner."

That was all he needed to hear. Shifting her underneath him, he covered her body with his, rocking his throbbing shaft against her moistened slit. He kissed her, devouring her mouth like a man who'd been abandoned in the desert without water.

There was no place he could touch without wanting to glide over it twice, no spot on her body that he kissed that he didn't want to go back and taste again. Desperation pulled at him, the need to possess every inch of her and never let her go.

She threaded her fingers through his hair. "I thought I'd lost you."

He licked her lips. "I know. But I'm stronger than you think. I'll always be here to take care of you, Katya. And our children and our pack. I'm never going to leave you. Not until we're both very, very old."

She smiled, love sparkling in her eyes. "I know. I have faith in you, Conner, and I'll never doubt again."

He closed his eyes as her words washed over him, her love for him a tangible thing. He didn't know what he'd done to deserve the love of a woman like Katya, but he was going to make damn sure to show her his appreciation every single day for the rest of their lives.

Starting now.

"Spread your legs for me, baby. I've been dying for a taste of you."

She whimpered and complied, planting her feet on the bed and raising her knees. He leaned up and looked down at her spread-eagled for his viewing pleasure.

Her nipples stood upright and begged for his mouth. Her belly quivered and her hips lifted in silent invitation.

The problem was he didn't know where to start. Nipples. Definitely nipples. He bent over and swiped his tongue over one hard peak, then the other, then began alternating one with the other until she reached for his head and pushed him south.

"Oh, but I love playing with these pretty nipples, baby."

"Lick me, Conner," she said, her breath coming in gasps.

"I am licking you."

She glared at him. "Not *there*. My pussy, dammit, and hurry!"

He laughed. "That was an alpha talking, for sure. Your wish is my command, Princess."

His tongue blazed a trail down her abdomen, stopping to slide inside her belly button. She giggled, the throaty sound more enticing than any moan he'd ever heard. He paused when he reached her sex, mesmerized by the look of her pussy. Her lips were pink, swollen and wet. Unable to resist, he licked her slit and circled her clit with his tongue.

She bucked against his mouth. "Do that again."

He did, and she moved her hips against his mouth, sliding her sweet pussy against his lips.

"I could eat you all night long, Katya." He slipped a finger inside her cunt, loving the way her muscles squeezed and pulled. It made him ache to drive his cock inside that tight vise until she squeezed every drop of cum from his balls.

First, his woman had to get off. Then it was his turn. Leaving one finger inside her pussy, he tunneled in and out while covering her clit with his mouth, licking back and forth like a ticking clock, following her nonverbal signals until he hit just that right spot and—

"Oh, God, Conner!" She flew over the edge, her cunt spasming around his finger, sweet nectar pouring out of her. He held onto her clit while she slammed her pussy against his mouth.

Once the spasms ended, her hips lowered and she lay there, eyes closed, panting heavily. He crawled over her and she opened her eyes, smiling at him. He slipped the finger moistened with her creamy cum inside her mouth. She lapped at it greedily, sucking the digit the same way she sucked his cock.

His shaft was jealous of the attention his finger received, but he'd be damned if he was going to dally any longer than necessary. There'd be plenty of time to feel her hot mouth surrounding his dick. Right now he wanted inside her wet cunt.

"Turn over, baby."

She did as he instructed, flipping over onto her belly. He slid two pillows under her hips, raising her ass high off the bed.

"You like fucking me this way, don't you?" she asked, craning her neck around to look at him.

"You know it. I'm a wolf, baby. I like it from behind." He leaned in and kissed her, then nestled between her legs and directed his cock toward that magic spot.

Katya was the magic in his life, what he'd been missing and had never realized it. And now, she was his forever. "My woman. My pussy. Mine."

The last word Conner uttered in a fierce growl, firing up Katya's nerve endings and making her desperate for his possession. "Yes, Conner. Yours."

He drove inside her, burying his shaft deep and hard. She drove backward to meet his thrusts, shockwaves of intense pleasure hitting every nerve ending in her body.

His movements were relentless. He leaned over her back, grabbing her arms and lifting them over her head, then pinning her in place so he could drive inside her harder.

"You ready to go again, baby? Because I don't think I can hold out too long. I need to spurt cum deep inside you."

His movements drove her clit against the pillows shooting sparks of need deep inside her. When he bent over and grazed her neck with his teeth, then bit down to hold her in place, she cried out.

Pain laced with the most exquisite pleasure imaginable took her over the edge.

"Fuck me, Conner! I'm going to come!"

He growled against her neck and sank his teeth in deeper. She couldn't move, could only lie there and feel every pulse of her orgasm as he pummeled her cunt with jackhammer thrusts until she screamed. Her climax raged through her, primal, savage, like the way Conner fucked her. Hot jets of cum spurted inside her, his life seed filling her.

She panted to catch her breath, the aftershocks of her orgasm still pulsing. Conner withdrew and lifted her off the pillows, collapsing onto his back and pulling her against him.

His eyes still blazed with the heat of passion, his body damp with sweat, the same as hers.

"I'm going to need another shower," she teased.

His lips brushed hers slowly, seductively, promising a night filled with sensual delights. "That's okay. I like shower sex."

She laughed and snuggled closer, resting her palm on his chest. She'd never tire of feeling the rhythmic thumping of his heart. It signaled life, and she was forever grateful to have been given a second chance at loving him.

"I love you, Conner."

"I love you too, Katya."

"I'm going to tell you that a lot." Never again would she hold her emotions inside. No matter what the outcome of the rest of her life, no matter what losses she had to suffer, she was going to make sure that she told everyone that she cared about how much they meant to her.

First and foremost her husband, her mate, her alpha.

"The moon's still glowing outside," he said, kissing her temple.

She sighed, feeling its magical power fill her, and knew that as long as she had her mountain, the moonlight and the man she loved, her life was complete.

"Sleep, baby. Tomorrow we have a lot of work to do."

"I know." She welcomed the tasks ahead. They had much to do to protect the Carpathian wolves, but with Conner at her side, she could do anything.

She closed her eyes, more relaxed and content than she'd ever been.

Destiny had brought Conner to her doorstep. Her ability to love him kept him here under the moonlight of the mountain she called home.

Their home.

Their mountains.

Their dynasty. A new life for all of them was about to begin.

*Enjoy an excerpt from:*
ANIMAL INSTINCTS

෨

Dressed entirely in black PVC leather, she strutted every inch of her goddess-like body in stiletto thigh-high boots, her silvery-blonde ponytail swinging from side to side as she approached. Full breasts swelled and threatened to spill over the top of the corset.

The closer she got, the more pronounced her frown became. Did she recognize him? Did she sense the same thing he did? Or was she really as clueless about what was inside her as he thought? If she knew, she'd have sought him out, he was sure of it.

The only reason he came here was because he didn't want to approach her at the clinic, and didn't want to scare the shit out of her by showing up at her apartment. He'd been watching her for weeks now, ever since he first picked up her scent at the clinic and realized there was more to Moonlight Madison than he'd ever guessed. And every time he saw her, he became more convinced she didn't have a clue about him, or about herself.

She stopped in front of him, her head tilted slightly as she scanned his body from head to toe.

The movement exposed her neck, one of his favorite parts on a woman. So tender, so sensitive, it aroused him just thinking about possessing that slender column of flesh, burying his teeth in her nape and holding onto her as he fucked her. The creamy expanse of her throat would look nice with a collar around it, too. As long as he held the leash.

He inhaled her sweet scent, thankful she hadn't tried to mask it with one of those cloying perfumes women sometimes wore.

"You're Blake Hunter. From the clinic."

He wasn't sure she'd acknowledge that she knew him. "Yeah."

"Figures," she mumbled low enough that the average person wouldn't hear. Then again, he wasn't an average person. He also wondered what she meant. She looked disappointed. As many times as he'd been to the clinic to pick up medicine for the refuge, he'd never spoken directly to her. She was always in the background doing something and his dealings had usually been with the receptionist or the doc. But he'd seen her. Knew she volunteered there and went to vet school part-time.

He still couldn't get over the transformation. Her typical worn blue jeans and an oversized T-shirt were night and day different from the sex bombshell getup she wore now.

Not that he minded her current attire. Either way, she excited him. A helluva lot as a matter of fact. He itched to throw her down on the floor of the lobby and shove his hard cock inside her, sink his teeth into the soft flesh of her shoulder and hold her in place while he rode her to a hard climax. He shuddered and pushed the beast away.

*Not yet.*

She moved to the reception counter and rested her elbow on the dark wood, looking perfectly calm and in control. The image she presented was a woman used to taking charge. At least externally.

Her brow lifted as she picked up the paper, scanned it and shot him a questioning look.

Yeah, he'd paid for her for the entire night. One hour wouldn't do it. He'd need the whole night and more with her. Then, if everything went as he hoped, they'd have an eternity together.

"Are you sure about this?" she asked, waving the receipt at him as she left the desk.

"Yeah."

"It's a lot of money."

"I *have* a lot of money. Let's get started."

Shrugging, she motioned him toward the hallway. "It's your dime. Follow me."

Blake sucked in a deep breath and tried to keep from drooling as he followed her fine ass down the dimly lit corridor. The corset thing and tight little panties she wore fit high over her curvy hips and narrowed across her buttocks, showing more than a little of her shapely ass.

His cock saluted its appreciation of her body. He didn't like overly skinny women. She had a woman's body. A real woman's body. Tits, ass, hips, legs that went on forever and thighs made for a man to ride between. Yeah, she was built perfectly in all the right places.

Places he'd like to lick, suck, bite and fuck. And he would. All in good time.

First he had to figure out how much she knew. If she hadn't realized anything yet, he'd just have to give her a little nudge in the right direction, because the moon was full, the beast within him was clawing to get out, and he wasn't going to wait one more goddamned minute to have her.

She might be the dominatrix in this place, she might cater to the kind of men who begged to be told what to do by a woman, but he was no more that kind of man than he was fully human.

As she led him back to what he assumed was her room, he smiled at the confident sway of her hips. Yeah, she thought she was in charge here, but he was about to turn the tables on her. Soon he'd have her cuffed, naked and pleading with him to fuck her.

His balls ached just thinking about giving her exactly what he knew she wanted, what she needed, what she craved. He knew enough about her to know that the lifestyle she led wasn't fulfilling her. Hell, he knew more about her needs than she did.

Something was missing in Moonlight Madison's life.

Him.

# Why an electronic book?

We live in the Information Age—an exciting time in the history of human civilization, in which technology rules supreme and continues to progress in leaps and bounds every minute of every day. For a multitude of reasons, more and more avid literary fans are opting to purchase e-books instead of paper books. The question from those not yet initiated into the world of electronic reading is simply: *Why?*

1. ***Price.*** An electronic title at Ellora's Cave Publishing and Cerridwen Press runs anywhere from 40% to 75% less than the cover price of the exact same title in paperback format. Why? Basic mathematics and cost. It is less expensive to publish an e-book (no paper and printing, no warehousing and shipping) than it is to publish a paperback, so the savings are passed along to the consumer.

2. ***Space.*** Running out of room in your house for your books? That is one worry you will never have with electronic books. For a low one-time cost, you can purchase a handheld device specifically designed for e-reading. Many e-readers have large, convenient screens for viewing. Better yet, hundreds of titles can be stored within your new library—on a single microchip. There are a variety of e-readers from different manufacturers. You can also read e-books on your PC or laptop computer. (Please note that Ellora's Cave does not endorse any specific brands.

You can check our websites at www.ellorascave.com or www.cerridwenpress.com for information we make available to new consumers.)

3. *Mobility.* Because your new e-library consists of only a microchip within a small, easily transportable e-reader, your entire cache of books can be taken with you wherever you go.

4. *Personal Viewing Preferences.* Are the words you are currently reading too small? Too large? Too… ANNOYING? Paperback books cannot be modified according to personal preferences, but e-books can.

5. *Instant Gratification.* Is it the middle of the night and all the bookstores near you are closed? Are you tired of waiting days, sometimes weeks, for bookstores to ship the novels you bought? Ellora's Cave Publishing sells instantaneous downloads twenty-four hours a day, seven days a week, every day of the year. Our webstore is never closed. Our e-book delivery system is 100% automated, meaning your order is filled as soon as you pay for it.

Those are a few of the top reasons why electronic books are replacing paperbacks for many avid readers.

As always, Ellora's Cave and Cerridwen Press welcome your questions and comments. We invite you to email us at Comments@ellorascave.com or write to us directly at Ellora's Cave Publishing Inc., 1056 Home Avenue, Akron, OH 44310-3502.

erridwen, the Celtic Goddess of wisdom, was the muse who brought inspiration to storytellers and those in the creative arts. Cerridwen Press encompasses the best and most innovative stories in all genres of today's fiction. Visit our site and discover the newest titles by talented authors who still get inspired - much like the ancient storytellers did, once upon a time.